Stranger to Love

Stranger to Love

Reece Brett

Black Lyon Publishing, LLC

STRANGER TO LOVE
Copyright © 2008 by JUDITH R. BRETT

Our books may be ordered through your local bookstore or by visiting the publisher:

www.BlackLyonPublishing.com

Black Lyon Publishing, LLC
PO Box 567
Baker City, OR 97814

This is a work of fiction. All of the characters, names, events, organizations and conversations in this novel are either the products of the author's vivid imagination or are used in a fictitious way for the purposes of this story.

ISBN-10:   1-934912-06-9
ISBN-13:   978-1-934912-06-5
Library of Congress Control Number: 2008931668

Written, published and printed in
the United States of America.

Black Lyon Contemporary Romance

Tender nights, tender moments, passionate love.
To my husband, who is my romantic hero.
To my muse for inspiration and support.

Chapter One

"Ever kill anyone with that?" The little boy on the stool next to Brent stared at the holster.

"No, that's only on television. Just more coffee, Rosie," Brent indicated to the waitress before turning to the boy. "Trenton, Maine is much too quiet to have much use for a pistol."

The woman beside the child caught Brent's attention. She wasn't a regular and May was too early for tourists. In the navy suit with a round-collared white shirt, she looked as if her grandmother had dressed her in a "nice girl" outfit. The staid ensemble didn't fit her generation nor did it fit the usual Tillie's Diner crowd. Her youthful pose of hooking her legs around the stool base revealed long, sensuous legs.

Brent quietly stirred his coffee and surreptitiously watched the woman. Although Tillie's was relatively quiet in the mid-afternoon, each clatter of coffee cups startled her. She glanced over her shoulder every time the bells rang indicating an arriving customer. Her hand protectively touched her son's back. What could make someone so nervous in this town?

The boy spun erratically out of control. As Brent reached to prevent his fall, his hand brushed the woman's. An electric charge passed between them. She jerked her hand away.

Something deep within him responded to her. He'd been a teenager since he last experienced an instantaneous physical reaction to a female. Maybe that's what happened when a man neared thirty—he developed yearnings for complete strangers.

"Welcome to Maine." He flipped his cop's hat on the boy's head. That momentarily stopped the boy's stool spins. "You visiting here long?"

The boy looked for his mother's approval before responding. "How did you know we were new?"

"I'm a policeman; it's my job to know the comings and goings of strangers." He immediately regretted his words. The woman ducked her head and turned her body away. He directed his questions to the boy. "Your dad getting a new job here in town? Are you moving here?"

The woman offered no comment to his question. She kept her eyes on the cup of tea in front of her. Brent noted she wore no rings on her hand.

"We're moving to the McDowells' house! I have a bedroom." As soon as he blurted out the information he checked with his mother. "I'm sorry, Mommy. I shouldn't have said anything."

Brent masked his reaction. What made the child check with his mother? Why was she so obviously protective?"

"Gabe, you're right for not talking to strangers, but he's a policeman." She smiled. The smile was neither warm nor friendly, but wary. He watched the interaction between the two. The child checked approval from the mother, but showed none of his mother's fears. She avoided eye contact. Instead she directed her comments as if she were talking to a spot beyond Brent's head. That piqued his curiosity further.

"We're moving to the McDowells' house soon."

"Seal Harbor. White house off the cul-de-sac."

"You do know the area." She finally faced him. Her faint smile faded.

"Maine isn't so populated that you don't notice things. McDowells haven't moved yet." He wanted another glimpse of her face and a real smile. Tiny wisps of auburn hair escaped the clip that tightly held massive curls. The loose tendrils contributed to her innocent aura. If he released that clip and could feel those curls trail softly through his fingers ... *Get a grip.* He didn't know her, had never seen her.

"We're staying in a motel. It stinks." The boy whirled on the stool. "I can't play with my trucks."

"Not much place for a boy. Cooped up in a motel room." He tapped his hat. The whirling stopped. "Maybe we could go fishing."

"Can we, Mommy, can we?"

She hesitated. Her grip on the counter tightened.

"Fishing is a part of Maine. I'd be glad to take him. It's safe. I've been going since I was his age. Room on the boat for you, too. You never let him out of your sight, I can tell." He placed his hand on her arm. The protective nature his sisters adamantly complained about kicked in. "I'm Brent O'Neill." He held out his hand.

"I'm sorry. We're from the city. People don't talk to each other much." She peeled her hand away. "I'm Marlo Saunders. This is Gabe."

"You won't be strangers here for long." He held back his urge to take her hand again or to reach out and touch her shoulder. Her tension cried out that here was a woman in need. He wanted to assist her and his job made that easier. "In Trenton, Maine, everyone helps each other. Here—" He scribbled on a napkin. "My number. If you need anything, call me."

"Thank you. We have lots to do before moving in." She placed her hand on her lap and out of his reach.

"You need anything? Want anything?"

"Clothes," she blurted then amended. "We left in a hurry. Left things behind. Does your wife shop anywhere nearby? Where do your children get their clothes?"

"Not married. No children," he said. "In town, not far from the motel is Quinn's department store. A popular spot for mothers in town. You could find clothes for both of you." He glanced down at her figure not adequately disguised in the suit. At best, five foot two and tiny. A man could easily pick her up and carry her.

He abruptly stood. He had to get out of here. This woman had avoided eye contact and had moved away from him. She hadn't shown any interest. Wanting to help a perfect stranger was part of his job. It had nothing to do with her smile or hair or legs.

"Thank you for your help." She hesitated.

"Gabe, you settle in. Meet here in one week and I'll take you fishing."

"That would be nice of you." A genuine smile subconsciously played across her lips. Her eyes flickered with warmth.

Without the worry lines and frowns, she was beautiful. Not the ravishing, unattainable beauty that appeared in magazines, but a beauty that made a man want to hold her and not let go.

"One week, Gabe. You be ready." He pulled his gaze from her to quiet the riotous thoughts he had.

The boy nodded eagerly.

"Call me if you need anything."

•

Marlo didn't call in that week. He looked for her in town all week, but only caught glimpses a beige Toyota with New Jersey plates, which was the sole foreign car in town. He meandered down the aisles in Quinns as if he were interested in T-shirts and socks, but bought nothing and saw no outsiders.

Questions swirled in his detective's brain: What caused her uneasiness? Where was Mr. Saunders? She guarded her son too closely. What was she expecting? To answer both of these, he wanted to see her again. Images plagued him: her tentative smile, the auburn wisps around her face.

A week later, Brent impatiently watched the clock and signed off at noon. The unfamiliar beige Toyota caught his eye as he arrived at Tillie's. The same car had been outside last week. He jotted down the tag number. It wouldn't hurt to check her credentials. A week before, he promised the little boy that he would be back. Brent pushed open the door at Tillie's. His gut tightened as he entered and saw a row of empty stools. Gabe's childish voice identified them as occupants of the last booth.

"How's the new house?" He knew the answer before he was seated. Gabe shredded napkins at the table. Marlo said nothing, but her shoulders slumped as she stirred the murky liquid in her cup. Her auburn hair now released from a clip flowed around her shoulders.

"Didn't move yet, huh?" When Rosie brought him a cup of coffee, he suggested, "How about an ice cream? Rosie makes the best sundaes with all the toppings." Gabe squiggled in the seat, but still looked over at his mother and said nothing. She nodded to Gabe's silent request.

"Did you get everything you needed at Quinns? I'm sorry about the house." He meant to console with a touch to the top of her hand. She flinched. He glanced at her face contorted as if in pain. Someone had been rough with this woman. What could he do to get her to trust him? She watched him like a tiny animal ready to leap to safety.

"You going to take us fishing?" Gabe said.

"Gabe Porter De—Saunders, don't be rude!"

"It's okay." His fingers tapped the tips of hers. "I have nieces and nephews. I know how they behave. I have the afternoon off. I'd love to spend it in the boat."

"Now?" Gabe's squeals drew the stares of patrons. Marlo looked down. She hated attention. She whispered in Gabe's ear and he quieted immediately.

"As soon as you finish that." Brent pointed to the immense sundae replete with chocolate pieces, whipped crème and three cherries equally spaced along the top. "Must have been a tough week. Motel's no place for an active boy," Brent said. "McDowells didn't leave yet."

"The deal fell through. They can't buy their new house so they're not selling that house."

•

Marlo avoided looking into his eyes. Escaping with Gabe had been a risk she thought she would handle, but she was a failure. Just as Tony had told her a million times, she wasn't capable of making good decisions. She thought McDowells' had been perfect, but now she had no other options. She swallowed back the sobs, which wanted to overtake her. So much to learn. She needed to be strong or she and Gabe wouldn't survive.

"Mr. Saunders looking for a new spot?" The policeman stirred his coffee without looking up.

"There is no Mr. Saunders." Marlo held her breath. Gabe was busy with his sundae and hadn't heard her lie. Luckily, Brent asked nothing more of her husband.

"Have anywhere to go?"

She shook her head.

"Didn't think so." The clearest blues she had ever encountered stared back with undaunted frankness. She was not experienced enough to know what to do now; she hadn't talked to many men. She needed to get his attention elsewhere. She couldn't afford questions about her situation.

"How many nieces and nephews?" she began weakly.

He paused. "Fifteen, I think. That's close enough."

"You don't have children. You seem to enjoy them." She bit her lip. Was that too bold?

"Never had time. Never the right woman."

Both became aware of the sudden quiet as if the whole town tuned in. Marlo stirred the butterscotch and ice cream. She looked for an escape. She couldn't afford attracting people's attention to her or to Gabe.

"Had enough? Let's go." Brent turned to Marlo. "I want to show you something."

She wasn't sure what to answer. His hand covering hers brought yearnings she hadn't known she had. This man was dangerous to her; she didn't think clearly when he was near. Yet, she longed for more of his attention, craved the reassurances his mere presence brought. If she thought about the danger of that, she wouldn't go. She refused to think about the past, but followed him.

"Come on." He led them to a green Jeep Wrangler. As they drove through town, Brent entertained Gabe with stories of fish and bears. He pointed out spots of interest to her as well. "In the summer months, we're mobbed with tourists. Shops thrive. In the winter, we're isolated. I have something I specifically want to show you both. Okay with you?"

She nodded. A peaceful collage of harmonious ponds separated by lines of tall, spindly pines depicted a postcard beauty. The outcroppings of rocks poking from the middle of the waters piqued her curiosity. Could one sit on those rocks and inhale the peace the scene offered? Having spent her life in the bustle of cities, the scenery kneaded the tension lines from her neck. Gabe was right—life in the motel was crummy. She straightened her shoulders. For the first time, she was answerable to no one. McDowells' had been a mistake, but not a disaster. She'd have to find a better place.

"It has a great fishing spot," Brent talked to Gabe seat-belted in the small backseat.

"Can I fish there now?" Gabe asked.

"Only if your mom agrees to cut off fish heads and scales and prepares a fish dinner." He looked at Marlo. His eyes danced.

Marlo found it tough not to let down her guard with this man. A weight had lifted just getting in his vehicle. His teasing, evident in his eyes, was contagious. "If your mom says it's okay, we'll fish, too. I have fishing rods there."

She relaxed against the seat. He was taking them to a fishing hole. It was safe.

"You know, I have a cottage on Frenchman's Bay." He glanced over Marlo. She sat up. "Big enough for the two of you. You could stay there until you come up with another place."

"I …"

To stop her argument, he continued. "You'll be safer at the cottage. Great fishing off the rocks." He included Gabe in the decision. He listed events, which included sightings of deer, moose and skunks.

Marlo watched Gabe's delighted smile. When he grinned, he looked like her brother. Only when he scowled did he bear any resemblance to his father, Tony.

Brent stopped in front of a cottage almost obscured by trees. He helped her out of the Jeep and led her down a path to the other side of the cottage. It faced a bay and the isolated shore of Maine.

"O-h-h." She didn't think beauty like this really existed anywhere. She stumbled down the first few steps of the path. A treasure beyond imagination. The water lapped the shore near a tiny cottage nestled amid pines. "It's lovely," she whispered. She tentatively walked around the corner of the cottage to view the coastline before her. "It's yours? You sure you want to share it?"

Gabe immediately scrambled down the slope to the shore.

"No one comes down the road except the neighbors. He can play without strangers interfering and without the danger of traffic. I'll only be here when you need me. It's yours until McDowells move or you find another place."

Before she could argue, he added, "Help me. I need to fix it up for my cousin. She's moving here. I have no idea how to convert it to a female inhabitancy. It's safer than the motel."

She shuddered. Every noise at the motel awakened her: car doors slamming, people's voices near their door. She couldn't keep Gabe under lock and key forever.

As if reading her thoughts, Brent continued. "Gabe has room to play, discover, fish. Gabe and I will try out the fishing." He opened the cottage side door. "You totally explore. Look in the rooms, in drawers, anywhere. Picture the two of you here and decide. No pressure." He held out the keys. She didn't take them.

Waves quietly touched the gravel and sand shoreline. Already Gabe jumped in and out of the wave edges. The afternoon sun shone through the trees. "We'll be down there." Brent pointed. She studied the man beside her. Sincere, trustworthy, he seemed. So far he showed no likeness to the same species her husband had come from. Brent's smile was genuine and sent glowing sensations down to her toes. She took the keys.

She watched his retreating figure before she entered the house. The side door led to a kitchen, which expanded to the family room beyond. The completeness of the kitchen with its shining pots hanging from an iron-ceiling frame stirred her baker's heart. What concoctions she could create here. She stroked the cool marble counter tops. This would be a perfect spot to roll out pie crust or cookie dough. The kitchen and the room beyond glowed as the sun poured in the floor-to-ceiling windows. Two doors in the family room led to a large deck. She watched Gabe and Brent untangle a fishing line.

He was a superb man to watch do anything. Even covered by his shirt, she caught glimpses of the strength and vitality as he cast the line deep into the waters. Yet, there was gentleness about him evident as he helped Gabe master casting. He certainly wasn't a giant of a man. Tony had been taller at six foot and a lot heavier. The mystique around Brent, the combination of strength and caring, captivated her. Were other men like this one or were men like Tony?

Taking this spot, involving him in their lives could be danger to her and to Gabe. Could she exist so close to him? She felt an enticing pull toward him. If her life had been different and she didn't have the past tainting her, she would like to know this man better. But he was a cop and she wouldn't afford to draw attention to herself. But this space ... she felt safe. This could be the home she had wanted. Did she dare say yes to this?

Did she have a choice? Maine was her safety net, she had to stay here. The motel was not a solution. She studied the room before her; a fireplace on one end offered a cozy welcome. An impressive, extensive library filled one wall of the family room. Although murder mysteries predominated, all types of books existed. Shakespeare, Yeats, Faulkner showed a wide interest and education. Little evidence existed that any woman had ever lived here. Did he go through so many women that none left their mark? Certainly that smile and those deep, endless blue eyes could attract many.

Upstairs, she discovered the master bedroom that occupied the entire second floor. Signs of this being a bachelor haven were everywhere.

Hearing Gabe's high pitched squeal, she raced to the deck off the master suite. He shouted as he pulled in a fish. It dangled and danced on the end of the line as Brent helped Gabe capture it. Gabe held up his fish in triumph and then ran toward the house. She arrived on the downstairs deck the same time the fisherman did. His face flushed, Gabe described his conquest as Brent laughed at the tale.

"Brent … Mr. O'Neill," he added when his mother frowned. "Says I can fish everyday. He'll let me borrow a pole. He'll show me where to fish. We are moving here, right, Mom?"

Marlo threw up her arms in mock resignation. "Certainly know how to convince me." She turned to Brent who leaned against the deck railing. The pine trees and the sun behind him created a frame for his appealing body. As he leaned back, he rested his leg on the picnic table in front of him. His sensuous grin and intense blue eyes created havoc inside her. She didn't know if she wanted to run away or move closer. "I don't know what to say," she stammered.

"'Yes' would suffice. You'll be doing me a favor helping me get it ready for my cousin."

Could she trust her instincts? She had made horrible mistakes based on her faulty judgments. She hesitated. This would be so much better than a motel for Gabe. So much more of a normal life. She nodded.

"You keep the key. I'll drive you back to the motel and your car. Help you load up and you can move in today. If you need anything here, call me. I'll be nearby."

For the next two days, Marlo busied herself with creating a home. No sign of Brent. No word from him. So much for her fantasies. He had helped in ways he never knew. She was grateful though disappointed with his departure.

She and Gabe slept in the little guest room on the first floor and avoided the master bedroom. It screamed Brent's image and an odor of musk and masculinity permeated the room. Her daydreams were already full of him. She didn't want her nights filled with his presence. His lean body, ready grin and strength fit any of the stories she had read in the grocery store lines which depicted the wildest fantasies. She had never indulged in such fantasies in the past. The brutal realities of Tony's world made imaginings absurd.

Fear nagged her still and the old habits died hard. She found excuses to be outside when Gabe ventured into the small patch of woods. She wouldn't let him beyond her sight. He would in time forget their past and its tensions, but she would never give up those images.

She attacked the job of making the cottage comfortable for someone else. She reminded herself not to get too attached. It was a temporary spot. Standing on the kitchen center island, she grasped the pot rack with one hand and attempted to replace worn screws.

"Anyone home?" Brent called.

Startled by an unexpected voice, she dropped the wire rack sending it clattering to Brent's feet.

"I didn't mean to frighten you, that's why I yelled from the doorway."

"It's your house. You can walk in." She pulled her hair out of her eyes with her fingers. "The rack's loose. The screws are." She had had daydreams about him, about conversations with him and now that he was here, she could only babble.

He agilely sprang to the counter beside her. "You screw, I'll hold it." Brent flinched. She hid her smile at his poor word choice. Maybe she affected his ability to talk, too.

"Here." He lifted her and held her in the air close to the ceiling where she fumbled with attachments. "This should make it easier."

Marlo's fingers trembled. The hands she had studied in Tillie's, the hands that had haunted her fantasies now held her waist. His proximity made it harder to work. If she leaned back, she would feel that muscular chest rubbing her back. She wanted to settle in those arms, feel his strength envelop her. She moved forward. She wouldn't rely on someone else. She had to learn about her own strengths. She finished the holder.

"I think that's an improvement." She faced those eyes and his inviting lips were inches away. He tilted his head and leaned down. She jumped to the floor, away from him and the urges. Grabbing the brush and cloth she had left on the counter, she rapidly scrubbed the oven door.

"The oven isn't that bad. I cleaned it not long ago."

She stood. Flipping her hair back with her fingers, she left smudges of dirt across her forehead. He gently rubbed the smudge with his fingers. His touch sent shivers down her spine. He rested one hand on the counter on either side of her, arresting any movement.

"You've done a great job so far. The ferns, the rearranging." He glanced around the kitchen and moved slightly close. "Anything you add. Save the receipts, I'll reimburse you."

His face was millimeters away. She stared at a spot on the floor. "I'll pay for it. We're living here."

The nearness of him, even the smell of musk and fresh ocean air that was part of him created a need she couldn't explain. A hot flush spread throughout her body. She couldn't afford to be this close. She ducked under his arm and fled to the sink. She ran cold water and took a deep cold drink.

"Jake Barber will be here nine AM to install an additional phone. I don't want you isolated without one. I'll pay installation and regular use. It's an improvement for me. You pay long distance bills."

She nodded. "Thank you. I hadn't thought about needing that."

Gabe ran out of his room. "Mommy." He stopped before them. "Brent ... Mr. O'Neill." He eagerly took Brent's hand. "I found a good fishing spot, wanna see?"

"Another day, Gabe."

"I'm going outside," Gabe announced before running out the deck doors letting them slam behind him. Marlo immediately walked around Brent and stood at the deck windows watching Gabe as he ran to the water's edge.

"He can survive for a few minutes without your surveillance." He rested a hand on her shoulder.

She tensed. "My son." The words came out sharp staccato. "You don't know. I can't stop watching."

He turned her to him. "Here in Maine, he can grow. Whatever makes you guard him so will fade. You can relax your guard, learn to lean on others. Learn I am not a danger." He squeezed her shoulder. "Look!" He spun her to face the doors. A red radiance stretched across the water beyond the trees.

"Oh." A tiny gasp escaped. Her fingers covered her mouth. "Oh. " The beauty of the sunset drove away any other thoughts. The sunset they could share. She reached behind to hold his hand. "I appreciate you letting me … us live here." Turning, she looked directly into his eyes. "Thank you for allowing someone you don't know share your private space, this cottage."

"I'm an easy judge of character. You need someone to believe in you." He wiped a smudge from her forehead. "I'll be around when you need me." He walked out.

She couldn't decide whether she was relieved or upset when Brent went home. Having him appear in her life created a glimmer of excitement. She couldn't afford a man in her life, but maybe she could acknowledge a friend.

The transition from tentativeness of a motel room to the stability of her own spot was easy. Rearranging flowers or baking an apple pie could be her decision. Placing a vase full of fresh flowers or moving the arrangement of chairs without asking anyone's permission was a revitalizing experience. She savored the freedom of being her own boss.

The openness of the cottage and the view she had from the deck captivated her. The sloping backyard led to the water's edge. Along the pebbled shore, she found her spot: a carved out rock made a perfect seat to view her new house as well as the ocean.

Marlo stared at the isolated shore. Tranquility and serenity seeped into her pores and blanketed her tension. Trenton was a good place. People moved at a different pace. Neighbors were friendly, open. She could start over here in a town away from the beaten path. No one knew she was here. Gabe was safe.

No sounds from Gabe. Her body tensed. He had been at the water's edge in his favorite spot.

"Gabe!" She stood frantically searching the edge of the woods. She had heard no one approach. Had he fallen in? "Gabe!" She ran down the knoll. "Gabe?"

"What's wrong? " Brent shouted from the top of the hill near the house. She had not heard his truck come up nor did she know he was arriving.

"Gabe's gone." She jumped to the boulder now surrounded by water and the incoming tide. She searched the water. Where was he?

"Mom." Gabe jumped from behind a nearby rock. "Got ya!"

Marlo rocked on the edge of the boulder. The last thing she remembered was Gabe's anxious expression and Brent's hearty laugh before she plunged into the icy water.

Brent's laugh greeted her as his strong arms pulled her to the safety of the shore. "You okay?"

Her breath came in gasps. Gabe was fine. The safety of Brent's arms soothed her panic. She leaned her head in the comfort of his chest. She willed herself to breath in and out in a steady rhythm. Nothing had happened. It felt so good to snuggle next to the warmth and security of Brent. Her heart pounded harder. He was so close.

Leaning against his hardened chest, the wet T-shirt afforded little distance. She wore nothing underneath it. Her nipples hardened as a reaction to the cold and the nearness of Brent. Pulling her closer, he peeled off his shirt and wrapped it around her. "It's too cold," he whispered in her ear.

His breath sent shivers down her back. The wet T-shirt and his warmth did nothing to cover the primitiveness of the feel of him. She could barely breath. The intensity of raw emotion took away all good sense.

"Before Gabe guesses more than his years understand," Brent said. "We'd better go to the house. I wrapped that shirt to cover you. Any more of the sight and the feel of you and a jump in the icy water won't cool me." He wasn't immune to their closeness. Nudging her toward the cottage, he said to Gabe, "We're going to try to get your mom warm and dry, then get dinner."

Gabe caught Brent's hand. "I thought it would be a surprise. I didn't mean to hurt her."

Marlo placed her arm around his shoulder and kissed the top of his head. He was safe.

"It's okay. Come on, Gabe, I've got new fishing lines. We'll check them while Mom showers," Brent said.

The warmth of the shower brought her shaking body back to reality. What happened to her? The closeness of a warm male body brought all her exotic impulses to overload. A suggestion, a move on his part and she would have touched him, kissed him. Couldn't happen. She couldn't make this mistake again. Too little experience with her own sensuality had to account for her reaction.

Dressed in a dry T-shirt and jeans, she opened the door to an awaiting Brent. "Are you okay?" Brent rose from the couch where Gabe had been curled beside him.

Marlo nodded. Gabe, still absorbed in the book he and Brent had examined, didn't notice his mother. He had none of the anxiety qualms that had enveloped her.

Feeling Brent's gaze on her, she met his eyes. "I'm glad you were here." The comfort offered by Brent's arms had been reassuring, but had also started an anticipation that left her restless.

Brent walked beside her and placed his hand on her shoulder. "You overreacted. It scared him."

"I thought he was gone," her voice cracked. She squeezed her eyes shut obliterating the echoes of Tony's threats. *Don't think of that. Don't let your past jut in now.* "I guess I am an overly protective mother." That was the best excuse she could offer.

His hand cupped her cheek, his index finger stroked back and forth before he spoke. "Something is fighting inside you. I'm not your enemy, Marlo. Let me help you."

The last four words were soft and tempting. Grabbing her hairbrush, she vehemently brushed her hair to have some physical activity to rid herself of his touch.

"Nothing." She flipped back her hair. "I have nothing to discuss."

Chapter Two

Marlo stood in the doorway watching Brent's retreating jeep. It bumped along the patched blacktop as Brent ripped down the roadway.

His touch swept away her fears. Burying her head in his chest enticed an aching she didn't understand. She had wanted to touch the hairs that beckoned from his unbuttoned shirt collar. What would those bare muscles feel like to her fingertips? But good judgment overrode her desires. Getting close to any one was dangerous. Letting a policeman too close was courting disaster. He had access to too many sources who would expose the evil person she once was. Anyone discovered the whereabouts of Marlo Saunders DeFalco and more importantly, Gabe, would jeopardize the cover her FBI agent, Miriam had so tightly woven.

She closed the door. The normal existence she desired for herself and or Gabe had limits. The cottage certainly was safer than the motel room. Here, she glanced around the family room, here she would create a safe, peaceful cocoon for both of them.

She strolled to the deck that stretched out the length of the family room. Gabe shook trucks from a plastic container. His notebook of beloved baseball cards lay on the wooden planks beside him.

Marlo walked down the steps of the deck to the grassy knoll leading to the water. She could see Gabe. His matchbox trucks rumbled across the openings between the planks. She followed the sloping backyard to the water's edge. Along the pebbled shore, she found her spot: a carved out rock made a perfect seat to view her new home as well as the ocean.

Marlo scrutinized the isolated shore. Tranquility and quiet encompassed her as if she were covered by warm, crisp covers. Tension eased from her shoulders. Trenton was a good choice. People were friendly, open. Gabe could thrive as a normal child. She could start a new life in a town away from the beaten path. No one knew she was here. Gabe was safe.

Movement at the edge of the brush caught her attention as a fox cautiously moved to the shore. The fox studied Marlo; she held her breath and didn't move. A kit moved out next to its mother. Another followed. The mother nudged them toward the water never taking her eyes off Marlo.

"It's okay," Marlo murmured. "I protect mine, too." The trio disappeared into the woods. Marlo smiled. A good place, Trenton, Maine. Tony was locked up far away. If she were careful, she could initiate a normal life here. If she observed others, she could mimic their behaviors. No one could trace her roots to New York City and Tony's lifestyle. She could develop a new persona to go with her new name.

Brent said no one remained strangers here long. She needed to mingle with other families to fit in. She couldn't stay secluded at the cottage that would be too noticeable. As long as she didn't let herself get too swept up by enticing Brent. Any attachments could cloud her judgments.

She walked to Gabe. "Come on, let's go to town. I need to buy groceries and linens."

"Can we eat there? In that restaurant? The one where Brent … Mr. O'Neill bought me a sundae."

Marlo bit her lip. "No. We'll try another place. Maybe I'll let you pick your dinner—even a hot dog."

Gabe tossed his trucks back in the container, then skipped to the car.

On the way past, Marlo glanced at Tillie's. No police chief's car. She wasn't sure if she was relieved or disappointed.

Gabe pointed to the advertisement inside the restaurant door. "Look, you get a poster and an orange truck."

Marlo sighed. This was the way families lived. Not the restaurants in NYC, but not with grim-faced guards either. Gabe chose his beloved hot dog and macaroni and cheese. After peering at selections in the buffet line, Marlo settled for a large spinach salad. She dipped the scoop in the hot bacon dressing and watched other mothers point out selections to their children.

As Marlo and Gabe headed to a corner table, Marlo heard the resonant voice. She turned slightly noting a lanky blonde rested her hand on Brent's shoulder. The woman leaned down and laughed, then said something to Brent. Marlo's stomach tightened and her desire for food vanished.

Of course, Brent attached himself to women. The attractive police chief was single. His seeming interest in her was the same attraction he would have to many women.

"Brent!" Gabe dropped his tray and bolted to Brett's side before Marlo could grab her son or silence him. Brent's smile of recognition almost melted her resolve to avoid him. He rose and followed Gabe to the table. With her back to the corner wall, she had no escape with the excuse of needing ketchup or spoons. The blonde closely followed Brent.

The blonde extended her hand. "Brent was just telling me about you. I'm Brent's sister, Alisha Shay."

A blush rose to Marlo's cheeks. His sister!

"We have a lot in common." Alisha nodded to Gabe. "I have an active seven-year-old."

Tongue-tied, Marlo merely nodded.

"When school registration starts at the end of the summer, we can go together. Why don't you let Gabe come over and play? Gabe and Jason will be in the same class. It would be great to let them get together."

"Sure, I don't—" Marlo felt the trickle of sweat wiggle down her backbone. The fine line between safety and danger depended on fitting in. Allowing Gabe to be an average seven-year-old was beneficial, but it exposed him to inherent dangers.

"It's okay," Alisha said. "You're invited, too. Brent vouches for you and Gabe. I know he rented his place to you. That's never happened. You can learn about me in a visit. I'm careful letting my son play with strangers."

"I wouldn't want to impose." She hadn't had friends to visit since seventh grade. Tony never let her go anywhere alone.

"Maine's a small place. I never get out. Wow me with tales

of the city life. Brent says you're from New York City."

Marlo flinched. How did he know? Had she told him?

Alisha tapped Gabe's hand. "Fishing, huh? Jason likes to fish. You and Jason need to meet before school starts."

"You have a son?" Gabe eagerly questioned Alisha about Jason as Marlo tried to quiet the ice ball in the pit of her stomach. This was the normal life she had wanted for Gabe. Friends. School. She'd have to register him for school, but how could she? She had no proof of identity. Using any real identification would be a dead giveaway to anyone looking for them. Too risky. Paper trails were too easy to follow. *He can't find us; he's locked …*

Gabe's insistent tapping on her arm brought her back to the safety of Maine and the warmth for the restaurant.

"Can we, Mommy? Go to school? Her son rides the bus. Will I? Can I?"

A bus. She never let Gabe beyond the stretch of her arm. *Tony's not here. He won't be. Let go of your nightmare.* "Yes, Gabe, you're old enough to ride a bus." She closed her eyes. *Please let me make the right decision. Gabe needs a life.*

Alisha's easy and open personality made visiting effortless.

•

A week later, Marlo sat at Alisha's breakfast nook with a cup of coffee in hand. Gabe and Alisha's son, Jason, played nearby "Last week, you mentioned New York City," Alisha urged. "Ever see a Broadway play?"

"Yes." She remembered the grandiose *Phantom of the Opera.*

"Oh? I read about Broadway, listened to CDs. I would give anything to see a real play."

Marlo laughed. "Broadway and New York aren't that far."

"When you have a seven-year-old, New York City is the moon."

Lights, sounds, the excitement of Broadway as she clung to Tony's arm had been an adventure. At seventeen, she had been bedazzled by Tony's riches, by his knowledge of life. Blinded, she had been so accepting and naive. As she noted the studied watchfulness of Brent, she buried those thoughts. Why had she ever told Alisha she had lived in New York? She had let her guard down as soon as she had a friend.

"Don't you think, Brent?" Alisha slapped him on the knees. "Marlo and Gabe should join us for dinner next Sunday."

"I don't know," Marlo said. She didn't want to force herself on either person.

"You can meet the whole family," Brent added.

"Your whole family will be there?" Marlo's voice squeaked.

"All five of my siblings and lots of kids. Gabe will love it. Crabs and spaghetti, games …"

"Please, Mom," Gabe tugged on her sleeve. "His brother has a fishing boat bigger than Brent's."

Brent whispered in her ear. "Come on. You can do this. Ask what you can bring."

"Can I bring anything?" She couldn't believe she was agreeing to this. A crowd. His relatives. The anticipation of a family outing was enticing, she had faint memories of her parents and her brother.

"What's your specialty?" Alisha asked.

"I love to bake desserts. What would you like? I know many recipes."

"Oh, bring a sampling. The more desserts the better."

Nothing prepared her for the onslaught of the O'Neill clan that Sunday. Overwhelmed by the masses of cousins, brothers, sisters, she sank against a tree and watched wave after wave of movement. Gabe immediately found his niche among the kids and deserted her. Brent rescued her with a quick squeeze of her hand.

He stood in front of her, blocking the confusion. "I'm glad you came here. She ducked under his arm and looked for Gabe's retreating figure.

Brent touched her face. "He's safe here. You watch him too much. Eight different pairs of adults. What could happen to him?"

Fear gripped her throat. She could list a multitude of possibilities. She grabbed a handful of grass. She looked down on the blades between her fingers. This was Maine. Tony and his men were far away not breathing down her back.

"Marlo, you're safe. Gabe is safe. Leave the mistakes of the past. Relax. I'm here."

He intuitively read her. Too close. This man was dangerous. She couldn't risk trusting anyone. What if he knew of her past?

"Uncle Brent." A tiny blonde twirled around Brent's leg. "Do you like her? Is she your girlfriend?" She clung to him. "They made me ask you." She pointed to a group of twelve and thirteen-year-old girls across the yard.

"Tell my nieces, I love only them." He struggled free of her grasp and sent her back to the other girls. He turned back to Marlo. He pulled her to her feet beside him. "I'm sorry. My family is bold, tactless and they make too much of any woman in my life. They're always on the look out for my mate."

"You're the only one not married?

He nodded. "Only male. Sister, Ericka, lives in Vermont. She's engaged. Marries next month. I look to be fair game for my sisters."

"And they think we're …" A blush rose to her cheeks. Matchmaking sisters.

"I'd like to go out," he said.

"What?" She caught her breath. The sudden warmth of the sun radiated through her body.

"Date … movies, dancing."

"Dancing? Out?"

He laughed. "You know dates. Like teens. I pick you up, we go out. You remember your teen years?"

"I never dated," she blurted.

"Never?"

She shook her head. "I worked, then married."

"I'll rectify that and take you out on your first date."

"With you? Out? A movie?" Her heart beat irregularly.

He nodded. "You usually go out with the one who asks you. So it's a date with me. Glad you haven't dated much. We'll have an initiation ritual this Saturday."

"Your family is all looking at us," she whispered. They had been deep in conversation ignoring the others.

"We're going on a first date, Saturday night," he shouted over his shoulder. "I need a baby sitter. I pay big bucks." Surrounded quickly by cousins and nieces, Marlo was separated from Brent.

Alisha pulled her from the babbling crowd. "Help me get desserts ready."

The quiet of the kitchen was resounding relief. The massive kitchen was warm and inviting with pots and pans hanging from the ceiling and flowers decorating sills. In a kitchen she was comfortable. In Tony's house, she ruled. The men stayed out. It had been the one place she was free.

"When you've raised six children, you need space. My mom reigns supreme in this room," Alisha explained. "I like to work here." Alisha lined up dishes and plates on a corner table. "Are you sure you want to go out with my brother?"

"I ... I didn't really say yes to date." Marlo circled staring at the herbs near a corner window. An eclectic disarray of chairs left in odd angles and placements looked like others had fled the room. The rest of the kitchen was immaculate. A real family spot. She sighed. She wanted a normal life like this. She liked the feelings Brent evoked.

Alisha paused as she placed desserts on a long, covered table. "Brent's avoided women since Christy. Real move on his part to ask you."

"Christy?"

"A real disaster in Brent's life ... I'll leave that to him to fill in."

"Brent's been real good to me. Good to Gabe." Just thinking of him close to her, sitting next to him at the movies, brought jitters.

"As a single mom, as any mom, you need time for yourself. Time to enjoy a life. If none of my nieces can baby sit, Gabe can spend the night with Jason." Alisha uncovered Marlo's whipped mousse. "If you make desserts like that, you'll get invited here a lot. What else did you bring?"

Marlo uncovered a fruit decorated flan. "I enjoy baking." Cooking and baking had been her outlets. Cooped up in an apartment, not allowed to go anywhere, guarded by Tony's henchmen, cooking had saved her sanity. Tony's boys had been willing to try her experiments, but Tony never praised her or sampled her efforts.

"Cook like that, I'll take you anywhere." Brent interrupted

and dipped his finger in the mousse. "This is incredible. You have a sitter for Saturday." He tasted her flan. "I'll clear your driveway of ice and snow for dessert as payment."

"Promise to be a good, I'll bake for you every week. I love it." She wiped the chocolate from the corner of his mouth. She smiled as the quips flowed off her tongue. She was flirting. A bit late to learn the trait, but being around Brent made her feel giddy.

"I am good. I promise." He moved around the table and wrapped his arms around her waist.

"I need to check with Mom." Alisha slipped out.

Brent leaned back so their bodies pressed together. "I want to date you … I want more." She attempted to squirm away from his arms, but one arm remained around her. "I'm not sure what frightens you, Marlo Saunders, but you can trust me. I won't hurt you."

Tony had cried when he hurt her the first time. The swellings of her eye had caused him to swear and rant at her. Then an hour later he pleaded with her to trust him. What was she doing here?

He refused to let go. He kissed her cheek. "You're in my arms, Marlo. You're safe. I will help you." His kisses began along her hairline, continued around her ear and along her neck.

She wanted to believe him. But it could put them in danger. "I can't, Brent. Don't. You can't help me."

His index finger stroked a line down her cheek. "It's a date. We can come home anytime. Agree to go out with me. Learn to trust me. Learn to trust someone."

A date. She wasn't leaving the state. If she didn't go out, find friends, she would be noticeable. Blending in with his big family could be a cover. "Where are we going on this first date?" The word "date" stuck on her lips. In her entire life she had never been on anything that would qualify as a "date."

"Movies, okay?"

She shrugged. Her mouth curved into a smile. A date. The smile crept across her face despite her attempts to remain detached. What could it hurt? Dating was normal.

"So?" He took her fingers into his hand. "You going to go

out with me? Saturday night? A movie and —" He let the "and" freeze in the air.

"Oh yes." Her smile widened.

"You have a stunning smile, when you let it appear." He stroked her upper lip. His nearness made her senses spin. The touch of his hand was warm and inviting.

"You guys gonna look that way at each other all night or what?" A niece walked in. "I'm hungry and Mom says we can't eat until you come out."

Holding her hand tightly in his own, they walked out among the questioning stares. Marlo positioned herself next to Alisha and helped cut dessert slices and dish out ice cream to the long line of children and adults.

Brent was unceremoniously pushed aside by the children intent on getting to the dessert table first. Brent observed her as she elicited smiles from each child she served. She greeted his siblings as they approached the table. She smiled easily. This outgoing, sociable Marlo was a side he hadn't seen. What brought out the other side? What made her so skittish as if she were a wild colt terrified of sounds and movement. Which Marlo was the real one?

When Cameron joined him, he was already holding his plate of chocolate mousse. Cameron licked the creamy substance off his spoon.

"Good dessert, huh. You look like one of the kids. Wipe your face." Brent handed him a napkin. "Marlo has a real talent here. Alisha and I are already inviting her to every outing just for her desserts."

Cameron swallowed his last mouthful. "She's moving right in the family, isn't she? So where did you meet her? She's not from around here."

"Chance meeting at Tillie's. She needed a temporary spot until she finds a house so she's staying in the cottage."

"She's not like the usual women you choose, and you aren't acting as distant as you usually do. What do you know about her? Not many strangers here in May."

Brent paused. "I know nothing" was not the answer he could give his brother right now, not after he had admitted giving her the cottage. He grinned and winked at his brother.

"Half the fun is exploring the questions and discovering the answers."

Cameron gripped his arm. "You're the police chief. Don't you think you should protect us all? You thought you knew Christy. Don't you think you should go slower here?"

Brent shrugged off Cameron's hand. "At five foot and tiny I don't think she is any threat. I learned my lesson there." He took Cameron's empty dessert plate. "Another bite of that flan is calling my name. I want dessert before my piggy family members gobble it all." Before Cameron could add any other precautionary notes, Brent left his side.

He had no clear answers to give any of his family about his involvement with Marlo. He had little answers for himself on why he was so attracted to her. He had discovered nothing when he had searched for information about her. It was as if she didn't exist. He should be vigilant, but he hadn't checked all his sources.

"Your desserts were a hit," he said to Marlo. He held out his plate. "Last piece for me."

She scooped a generous portion onto his plate. "I wasn't sure what you liked. I thought of saving you some." Marlo steadied one hand by leaning it on the table. Marlo had watched Brent as she helped out with desserts. Even dressed in casual clothes of a shirt and slacks, he was an impressive figure. He didn't have the imposing trappings of a policeman's uniform. The irresistible connection she had felt for him that first day at Tillie's had tempted her into staying at the cottage. His enticing body and endearing concern for her had her agreeing to dangerous compromises, like being here with his family. Would they be so nice and hospitable if they knew of her past? Brent shifted his weight.

"You survived my brothers and sisters. What do you want to do now?"

"Helping has been fun. I was glad to have something to do. Can I get you with anything? Do you want anything else?"

"Just 'yes' to the date."

Her hand stopped mid scoop. She didn't dare look up or he'd see her excitement. Miriam told her to start over, to try new things. Miriam had helped with so many adjustments.

She had advised she leave that past behind. Thanks to Miriam she could risk changes such as a date. She could feel Miriam's approving nod. "A date could be fine, Brent."

Brent held out his hand. "Come on, Sunday picnics and games are a tradition. We won't force you to participate, but you might as well see how scary my family is. Some competition, cards, games, music. You can play or you can observe." They walked across the lawn. Groups already formed in preparation for the late afternoon. Gabe was immersed in a tag game and didn't even notice his mother.

Marlo watched from the sidelines as the cards and the one-liners flew across the table with equal speed. She had never seen a family so close and so full of life. She had faint memories of a family dinner when her parents had been alive. Dinners at Aunt Mabel's in her teen years had been painful. None of her family experiences had the noise, the laughter or the chaos of Brent's family. Although she and Brent had little time alone the rest of the day, he left her with assurances he'd pick her up Saturday at seven.

When the phone rang later that night, she anticipated his changing his mind. No one was there. She only heard a sharp click.

•

The anticipation of Saturday evening left her hands clammy as she awaited Brent's arrival. She felt like the adolescent waiting for her first date, could barely button her shirt with her shaking hands. She had watched others with their dates saunter past her aunt's house, had covertly watched as they talked and kissed in the booths where she worked as a waitress. Aunt Mabel had discouraged any teenage interest in boys as a frivolous occupation, which brought only trouble. No dates until now. Marriage, babies, but no dates. Brent and his niece arrived promptly at seven.

"Hi, I'm Karla, Cameron's daughter," the niece announced. She glanced over at Brent who was talking with Gabe. "Uncle Brent is real nervous. He stalled his car three times on the way here."

Brent leaned against the door frame. Marlo felt her pulse leap with excitement. She was extremely conscious of his appeal and her own budding interest. What was he expecting tonight? They weren't teenagers with the same constraints.

"Come on." He led her out by the arm before she could list all the emergency situations Karla might incur. "She's baby sat before. She's survived Jason." In the car, he listed all the movies playing in the vicinity. "What do you like to watch? Action? Horror? Romance?"

"Not sure." Suddenly shy, she didn't know what to expect. Was she to decide a movie? What should she say? She wanted him to be happy not dread going out. "I don't look at many movies except Disney and that's on TV and only ones with a G rating. I'm a beginner here," she finally admitted.

Her confession to watching rated movies brought a hearty laugh. Marlo's shoulders relaxed. Her tension dissolved.

"Okay, I'll add to your education. You've grown beyond PG. We'll start with romantic suspense. Don't think action films will interest you."

He had no idea how much he contributed to her education when he held her hand in the movies. The warmth of his palm enticed her senses. The romantic embraces in the movies made her restless and nervous. Life in the movies had been distant. Could those scenes be real?

Dating, sitting in a movie theater with a male was foreign. It was as if she were in a movie viewing the changes in her life. At twenty-seven-years-old, she was experiencing life for the first time and life was wonderful. Brent's fingers intertwined with hers, sharing popcorn and brushing away a stray kernel from the corner of his mouth, the warmth of his thigh touching her was new and exciting. Dark, hairs curling out Brent's unbuttoned collar invited her touch. What turned him on? What intensified a man's passion was a mystery. A mystery she'd like to solve. Brent still held her hand after the movies as they walked down the street.

"Well?" His looking down at her with wicked grin prompted a smile. "Romantic suspense a good choice for you?"

"Makes you believe romance is possible and occurs in everyday lives." Marlo matched her step with Brent's.

Brent stopped in the middle of the sidewalk forcing other moviegoers to walk around. "You don't think romance exists outside of movies? That was a pessimistic statement."

"Romance works on the screen. In reality, most of is in your mind. Men and women fulfill needs in each other's lives." She shrugged.

"Maybe fate moved you to Trenton so I could show you romance is alive and a part of everyone's life. You just haven't been with the right people." With that he opened Tillie's door with a flourish shaking the bell loudly announcing their arrival to the crowded diner. Marlo felt the eyes on her and heard murmurs behind them as she followed Brent to a booth. The small town had much to say about their police chief dating.

"Not much in town after hours," he explained.

Marlo picked at the pie and slowly sipped her coffee. What now? The adolescent stirring started at the movies continued. His words echoed in her ears, the right people. Certainly the right romantic people had never existed in her life. Certainly, none of the people she had know were anything like the movies. None were like Brent of his siblings either. If she were careful, maybe she could keep up friendship with Brent and his family. The evening had proven better than her imaginings about dating.

What happened next? She tapped the pie crust with her fork tip. Dates made out in cars at the end of the evening or was that only in 1950s movies? Would he take her in his arms? She wanted the closeness of him.

"I like Gabe," Brent said to start conversation and close out the suffocation he felt by others keying in on their date. "Didn't expect him to be so eager to do and try things. He's not the same as my nieces and nephews."

"Your family is so close. I've never had much family life. Big families are …"

"Overwhelming. Suffocating. Demanding."

"But you love it, it shows. All of you act together as if you were one. You have fun in your games and even talking." Her last statement, she said a little too wistfully.

"Do you have any brothers and sisters?"

"A brother. I haven't seen him since I was ten. I don't even know where he is." She quickly changed the subject. "Gabe adores you." She sipped her coffee. "There haven't been many males in his life."

He ate a piece of pie working carefully on the right word. Pieces of her life didn't fit together. He wanted to know more of her past. What happened to the brother? And for that matter what happened to Mr. Saunders. She and Gabe carefully eliminated him from conversation. "Life wasn't easy?"

"No, it wasn't. Raising Gabe in the city when he was so young. He had no friends nearby. Just adults." She concealed the truth poorly. Her reluctance to talk, to let him in on her past disturbed, but not in the way it should. Her uneasiness only spurred his need to come to her aid.

"Gabe likes Maine, especially the fishing. The move had been good."

"You look good. I mean, better. The move helped."

She touched his hand. "It is better. Our move to Maine, meeting you at Tillie's—was fortuitous for us. We wouldn't have made it without you."

"The job of a policeman. Keep new inhabitants content and eager to stay in Maine."

"No." She smiled and continued to touch his hand. A warmth flowed between them. "You're more than the neighborhood police to us. You've made the move easier." Embarrassed by her admissions, she stopped.

"Let's go," he said as he placed money on the counter. He drove to a sandy inlet. The moon hung overhead. A bench under the trees completed a romantic picture rivaling the movie just seen.

"My thinking spot." He patted the bench next to him as he sat. "I wanted to share it." The comfort of his nearness and the intimacy of an uninterrupted moment set her heart pounding. The land jutted out into the water. The water lapped the shoreline.

"Under no circumstances are you to tell my family of this spot." He glared, but the delighted, dancing blue eyes took away its effect.

"Don't they know about this?" She sat. His nearness magnified the scene. She was sure if she sat closer, even he would be able to hear the beating of her heart. She wiped her palms on her skirt.

"Never brought anyone here before. My spot to get away from siblings, nieces, nephews. Everyone. But I wanted to share it with you."

She should move off this bench. Her body warmed with the intensity. If she touched him, would she be too forward? She glanced at him—he was studying her. "I'm honored. And for the right price I can be bribed into not telling your family."

His smile made her braver. She moved closer until their bodies touched. His face was inches away. What should she do now? She swallowed and licked her lips. She wanted to kiss him. He was so close. If she just turned her head ... She closed her eyes.

She felt his lips touch hers so softly it was almost as if she wished it. Then his tongue tantalized her upper lip, this was much better than a wish. She leaned toward him. Brent's hand rubbed the back of her neck and pulled her toward him as his tongue darted along the inside edge of her mouth. She whimpered. Tentatively, her tongue touched his, then sparred with the tip of his tongue. She leaned closer for more body contact to ground her. Instead the feel of his chest pressing into hers made her soar higher. His fingers tangled in her hair and gently kneaded the back of her head. She stroked the top of his shoulders. He felt magnificent; the strength in his shoulders could protect her from anything. She abruptly pulled away. She couldn't do this. No one could ever protect her.

His hand stayed entangled in her hair. Her breath came in short gasps as she watched his tongue move across his bottom lip. The sensations he had just elicited with that tongue had been her undoing. For a moment she had forgotten who she was and how dangerous this man was to her seclusion.

"No ... I can't do this ... I'm not good at this. "

Brent stood. "Your kisses are devastating. Any more of that and this will be an unforgettable first date for both of us." Holding her hands in his, he pulled her up beside him. "We need to take this slowly. We need to know more about each other."

She shook her head. That was the very thing she needed to avoid most. He couldn't know about her. Being with him was a mistake. He created needs within her she couldn't fulfill.

"I want this to be just a beginning. I want to do more."

She shook her head. She couldn't trust herself around him. She wanted more. She wanted to know what it felt like to be a woman. To be a woman a man wanted. But she didn't dare attract his attention. She didn't dare let him know more about her.

"Please, Brent. I need to go home." She straightened her skirt. "I need to check on Gabe. He's not used to me going out."

Brent opened his mouth then closed it. He nodded and merely held her hand and walked back to the car.

Later that night restlessness engulfed her. She paced the deck facing the woods and the water beyond. Tony had never kissed her like that. She had so little experience with men. A simple kiss turned her inside out. She wanted to see more of Brent, but was afraid she would want more—more kisses, more touches—all of it. That would not be keeping her distance.

She darted inside quickly to answer the ringing phone before it awoke Gabe.

Brent's low husky voice said, "Hope I didn't wake you. I couldn't sleep. Your kisses pack a wallop, ma'am. I can't sleep."

"I can't sleep, either."

"I need to elicit a promise from you."

She hesitated and wound the phone cord around her fingers. "A promise?"

"You can't reveal my hiding place to my family. I need some space from the hordes of sisters. What bribe can I offer?"

"Bribing an officer? That could get me in trouble." She smiled. Joking was a new trait that still felt strained.

"How about we make it a steady date just for assurances."

She sighed and bit her knuckle. Reality ended the banter. "I can't, Brent. You don't really know me."

"That's usually why people date. What ever makes you nervous, you can share with me. You stayed here for a reason. I don't want to take the place of the man you loved, just share some time. Let me show you Trenton."

"Brent, you can't know. There are things about me …" She was revealing too much.

"Trust me. I will learn only what you tell me. I won't have to study you and your past to get to know you."

She gasped. She couldn't arouse his suspicions. She needed to stay in Trenton.

"Let me show you around Trenton, go out places for a month. Then you'll know if you want to stay in Trenton and you'll know if I'm trustworthy. And I'll know if I can trust you not to tell my sisters where I disappear. That's a spot that's been a savior since I was ten."

She smiled at his plea. She needed to learn about the area. If she kept Brent around, she could control what he learned. She shook her head. All that was just an excuse. She wanted to see him again.

"Is your silence an agreement that we have a date?"

She laughed. "Okay. A date. You can show me the area."

"And I can show Gabe the best fishing spots?"

"Oh, using my son." She twirled the cord. "He would love that, Brent." At least she could assure that Gabe had a good male to imitate. A police chief had to be a good person.

"I'll stop to see you tomorrow," he promised before hanging up.

She stood on the deck looking out at the water. She could try a normal life for both her and Gabe as long as she didn't get too involved. She had to keep up appearances, and maybe those appearances could be a reality for them.

Chapter Three

She hummed the next morning as she prepared breakfast. As soon as the sun was up, she and Gabe moved outside.

"Maine is a great place, huh, Mommy?" Gabe played on the shore's edge. Marlo enjoyed the quiet and stillness of her seat upon her boulder nearby. A different path her life had taken in Maine.

"Mommy, I found a cave, wanna see?" With Gabe's insistent tug, she followed him to the edge of shore. Midway between the woods and the water, lapped by gentle wave of low tide, a string of boulders served as the perfect hiding spot for a small boy. She affectionately tousled Gabe's hair. Gabe had a new life here and the freedom to explore included him. She had learned to let go a little. He had slept at Jason's and had gone with Jason's cousins to Tunnels. Life held new adventures.

"Mommy, are you watching?" Gabe tapped her arm. "See that boat. Wave. The man is waving at you."

"No, Gabe, don't." She tried to keep the panic from her voice. "Duck. It's a game. Hide." She yanked him to safety behind the rocks and studied the boat. A small motorboat idling across from her cottage, was distant enough not to run aground, but close enough to watch her space. Chills rose across her back. Apprehension overwhelmed her. What was it about the boat? Paranoia over her past? Or her protective instincts warning her?

"Mommy, that man was looking for something. Maybe we should help." Gabe offered from beneath her.

"Stay there."

"Yesterday, he looked with binoculars. He must not have found it."

"Yesterday? You saw the boat yesterday?" She stooped beside him. "When Gabe? " She grabbed him by the shoulders. "Why didn't you tell me?" Gabe's blanched expression, his wide-eyed focus rattled her motherly instincts. *Take a deep breath. Don't panic Gabe.*

Gabe shrugged out of her grasp. "Lots of boats out there. The man had binoculars. He watched the shore. He looked in the woods."

She stood. With her hands on her hips, she glared at the boat. A brave stance if anyone on board could see her. She stared down the boat until it moved away from her view. Then grabbing Gabe by the shirt, she raced to the cottage. She pulled down the shade and crumpled on the couch.

Occupying Gabe with a video, she paced in front of the shaded porch doors. Now what? Pack and leave? She couldn't always run. She couldn't always wait. Should she ignore her vow of silence and call Miriam, her FBI contact? Miriam would at least know if Tony ... *Please don't let it be Tony.* Several minutes passed before she was able to get through the rigmarole of passwords and security to Miriam.

"I'm sorry, Miriam is not here. Why are you calling?" Linda, Miriam's secretary and watchdog gruffly demanded.

This was against the protocol set up by Miriam, but she needed to know. "Where is she? Did she say anything about Tony Defalco?"

"I can't answer anything. You'll have to talk with Miriam. She'll be back in two weeks. Any messages?"

Marlo inhaled sharply. Not there. "No, no messages." She hung up. She needed reassurances Tony was still behind bars.

The boat was gone, but her sense of foreboding was not. Her fledgling instincts were shaky. Programmed by her aunt and then Tony, she had followed what others said was good or bad. Could she trust her feelings? When Marlo was a child, her mother had said she was a good judge of people and situations, but her mother died before she met Tony.

"Mommy, do I have to watch the video? I'd rather be outside."

What was she doing to her son? Would he ever have a normal life? She peered out the window. Nothing. She straightened her shoulders. "Let's go into town," she suggested. "We'll go to lunch, the grocery shopping. Okay?"

"I'd rather play," he mumbled as he dragged his feet across the gravel to the car. She cast furtive glances to the ocean. No boats. No binoculars.

"Think Brent … Mr. O'Neill will be there? We haven't seen him today. If we went to Tillie's Diner, we might see him." Gabe scrambled in the front seat beside Marlo. She helped him fasten his seat belt.

She ruffled his hair. "You get to pick the lunch spot. We'll keep an eye out for Brent." She wanted to see him, too. Seeing him everyday would be okay with her.

"Think Daddy would like Brent?"

Marlo gripped the steering wheel. "We won't discuss Daddy, remember? We promised, okay?" Could she ever promise him a normal life?

Strangers didn't exist in Trenton. Through the manipulations of Alisha and Brent, she had met many. Shopping in the grocery store was a social event. Stopping to talk to other shoppers was the norm.

"What do you feed picky boys who would eat hot dogs and apple sauce all day every day?" Alisha appeared at her elbow.

She laughed. "Invest in a hot dog company. Gabe picks at one meal, then gobbles the next." Brent's appearance interrupted the conversation.

"I want to see you," Brent said. The touch of his hand on hers made her forget her conversation with Alisha.

"Jason wants Gabe to come with us. We're going to the beach to play." Alisha said.

"Oh, I don't … " She looked at Brent.

"I want to take Marlo on the boat. Okay with you? You can manage both boys for a while?" He asked his sister. "A boat ride, okay?" He looked at Marlo.

Marlo glanced from Brent to Alisha. Could she leave Gabe alone? He rarely was more than an arm's length away. It was the only thing that assured his life. Would he be safe without her? She had left him with a baby sitter, he had survived.

"It's okay." Alisha said. "Single moms need time. Go. Gabe will be fine. We'll get lunch at a hot dog stand. We'll bring him home about one."

Marlo wanted the normal childhood — going with friends was normal. Obsessing about motorboats and strangers on a big bay was abnormal. Maine was a safe haven. Today's boat had unnerved her. If she wanted to appear normal and wanted Gabe to grow up like other boys, she needed to act like other moms. Other moms didn't panic over a man with binoculars. She took a deep breath. She nodded. Jason and Gabe's cheers rang throughout the grocery. Before she could change her mind, Brent ushered her through the checkout line and had her on the boat.

She sat on the cushion near the steering wheel. Never in her years in New York or even in the last few months would she have pictured this. She shopped by herself at a grocery and had friends to talk with. Okay, so her only friends centered around Brent's family, but Alisha talked with her mom-to-mom. Gabe was out with a friend and for the first time since his birth, since her marriage, she was doing something for herself.

"What is that smile for?" Brent unwound thick rope on the floor before her.

"I'm just enjoying the view." As she watched Brent start the boat and cast off, she nestled back on the boat cushions. Sharing his world, going out on his boat that was a part of him was her adventure. Watching him move effortlessly about the boat, a second nature to him, was enticing.

She marveled at the man now stripped of his jacket and dressed in a T-shirt and jeans. Muscles flexed as his hands which expertly handled ropes and steering wheels. The jeans sensually hugged his hips. She could enjoy time with him and the view. A beautiful day stretched before her. Her day. No one would take these pleasures from her.

The sails filled with wind and the bounce of the ship as it skimmed over the bay accented her pleasant feelings.

"Wanna try your hand?" Brent stood at the helm. "Come on, it's easy. City girls should learn the waterways of Maine. This is the helm. Deck. Port is left. Starboard is right." Brent rattled terms and pointed to spots.

She stood in front of him, his hand beside hers on the wheel. The wind blew her hair out behind her. Brent's body stood dangerously close. She could feel the warmth of him. His arms encompassed hers as he directed her hands on the wheel and pointed out sights along the shore and water with his hands. Her body developed its own heat with his nearness. Directing the boat across the water, the sprays sprinkled her face and the breeze caressed her cheek, as he held her close. She wanted to dance across the waters, shout at the top of her lungs with the exuberance she felt exploding within. This was the way life should be.

"Look!" Brent's arm stretched over her shoulder ant pointed out in the water. She studied the spot. Nothing. Then grey forms, glistening with water and sunlight burst out side by side. She looked over to Brent not understanding what he noted.

"Dolphins. Keep watching. There's more. Watch to the port side." He glanced to the left and pointed. Marlo ducked under his arm and raced to the side as four dolphins arched and swam past within a few feet.

"Dolphins? That close? And not in an aquarium?" She barely whispered her questions. "Dolphins? Free? Free to fly through the waves."

Brent smiled at her astonishment and the tenderness that touched her features. He turned the boat. "I can't crowd them. Their space is protected. But if you watch the water, they'll surface again."

Marlo leaned over the railing intent on motions in the water. A childlike mask of astonishment and delight showed in her face. Who or what had tampered with her spirit leaving her distrustful and unsure? Brent wanted to give new adventures, open her life to new delights, give her experiences which brought out the excitement and passion he saw written on her face just then.

She scanned the horizon for more movement. Her eyes danced with excitement. Her features became more animated. Laughter bubbled forth. She returned to his side and rose to her tip toes looking ahead. Her excitement was infectious.

He draped one arm across her shoulders. They stood hip to hip. "Maine is a wonderful state," he whispered in her ear.

She rested her head on his shoulder. "Brent, this has been a perfect day."

The wistfulness in her voice tugged at his gut. Her silence about her past, her watchfulness and distrust of people made her different and he surmised she had had few perfect days. He wanted to give her many.

"There!" He turned the boat and pointed at the water sprout in front of them. "Whale."

Marlo squealed and jumped up and down like a thirteen-year-old. Still clinging to his arm, she leaned forward as if she could make the boat faster. They neared the last sighting, Brent idled the boat and they both peered at the choppy waves.

"We won't hurt it getting this close, will we?" She clung to his arm, her fingers digging in his forearm.

"I won't get too close. They're savvy. Many boats come out to watch them. Look, he's showing off." A few yards away a black hump arched out of the water. A gasp came from Marlo.

When the waters quieted, she threw her arms around Brent's neck. "Oh Brent, thank you. That was wonderful!" With her sleeve, she quickly wiped away tears.

"What's wrong?"

"I never knew I would be so happy. What a day!"

"Day's not over yet." With his arm wrapped around her waist and her arm still around his neck, he steered to quieter waters. Beneath his arm, he felt her heart pounding. Fire brewed in her eyes—a fire from deep within. Passion. Marlo had a passion for life. What would ignite that passion other times? What else could he give her to break through her defenses and bring about her refreshing delight in the world around her. Cameron was right; he knew little about her, but Cameron was wrong if he thought Brent would wait to become involved with her.

Brent directed the boat to the middle of the bay. The ocean vastness lay dead ahead. Once isolated, he turned the wheel and brought in the sails. He hoisted an anchor over the side.

"We can just stop like this in the middle of the ocean?" Marlo asked.

He stretched out on the deck beside her. "The anchor will hold us. We can enjoy the peace." He patted the deck beside him. "Come on down, we can see what birds we can spot."

He maneuvered her around until she sat between his

outstretched legs. Her back leaned against him and his arms hugged her close.

She squirmed on the deck until she was half-turned toward him. "And you've enjoyed this your whole life. You've always lived here?"

He nodded. "The ocean makes you appreciate how little control mankind has. And how lucky mankind is. Lucky that only a few special people have discovered Maine."

She sighed and looked out over the water. "A special place."

The tip of his finger traced a line down the side of her cheek. "And you are a special lady." Taking her cheeks in his hands, he brought her face close to his and kissed her. First, encircling her lips with his tongue, then teased the sides inside her mouth. Her soft moan encouraged him to explore her body. His hands stroked down her arms, then his palms spayed across her stomach. She quivered at his touch, but she did not move away. If he didn't stop soon, he would have her at the bottom of the boat beneath him. So much for his resolve to give her time. When he stopped, she still clung to him. A moan escaped her lips.

"I wanted to do that in the grocery store."

"We would have scandalized Trenton." Her world spun around her as Marlo struggled to get a hold of reality. Her grip on his shoulders eased, but she still clung to him. If she let go, would he and this moment disappear? Were these sensations part of her life or was this some fascinating dream?

"Holding you, watching you discover that whale, I wanted to kiss you then."

She moved closer, resting her head on his chest. "I will never forget this day."

The passing of a large motorboat directly across the bow rocked the boat. The pitching separated them. The larger boat quickly surged around them sending sprays of water, dousing them both. Brent's boat rocked with the intensity of the waves. Brent swore under his breath, grabbed the mike from the cockpit. "Nicholas, a boat out here, cut across … We're a sail boat. They were …" His words drowned in her ears.

Waves of fear doused whatever flames Brent had inspired.

That boat was the same one that lingered outside her shore. Someone was too close. She dug her nails into the trim on the deck and gulped air. She leaned down and closed her eyes to shut out the dizzying sensations, which made it difficult to think. Someone was close and watching.

She had been so busy enjoying herself convincing herself this was a normal life, she had let down her guard. What was wrong with her? A smile, a warm male and her desires swept her away. She had to be in control and vigilant.

"Didn't see the numbers. Coast guard after them ... Illegal passage." Brent flipped off the mike and left it dangling near the helm. He stood in front of her. "Who's in the boat?" His blue eyes pinned her to her spot. "What do you fear? Who was that?" he demanded.

"I don't know... anyone here." She studied a distant speck on the ocean. She couldn't look at Brent. "I—"

Brent knelt in front of her. "You're frightened of something. Always looking over your shoulder. Tell me, Marlo." He ran his fingers through his hair. "Tell me so I can help."

He reached for her hand. She jumped aside. He wasn't Tony. He hadn't followed a question with a blow. She settled back to a sitting position. "I don't know who's in the boat, Brent." She studied her hands. She didn't know, but her gut said that show was for her. She was afraid to tell Brent anything about the boat this morning, about her fears now.

Brent waited for several moments, then moved to the helm and started the boat. He said nothing. When they reached the dock, Alisa, Jason and Gabe were waiting.

Gabe's chatter filled the silence on the ride to the cottage. Marlo stopped at the pathway leading to the Brent's cottage. "Thank you." She faced Brent. His blue eyes were flat, unfeeling, his face a stern mask. "I've never had a day like that." She hesitated. "It is one I won't forget." She took Gabe's hand and led him through the cottage door.

Brent pounded his palm on his steering wheel. That woman elicited such a mangle of reactions. The Marlo who jumped up and down and squealed with delight over dolphins, thanked him for an unforgettable day—just a simple day on Maine's waters—didn't fit with the same woman who jumped in fear over sounds, or who hovered so vigilantly over her son.

His training said don't trust her, keep investigating until you find something about her. His gut reaction said she was a woman in trouble who needed a friend and needed help.

He headed back to the station and his computer. Jeffrey, a private investigator in Portland, had more resources, more links. He'd call him. Before this connection continued, he needed more information.

Chapter Four

Marlo sat stirring her coffee, then walked outside along the shore and sat on her rock. A brief phone message from Brent merely stated that he had been called away. She had heard no more. Had she angered him and that was his kiss-off statement? Had she just been a passing fancy and he was no longer interested? She like the attention from Brent, liked his touch. She had so little experience with men, she wasn't sure what to think or what she should do.

"Mommy? My book is frayed. Its pages and the cards are unraveling." Gabe held up a well-worn notebook, his only attachment to his father. She wanted to dump it in the bay in a storm and watch it drown. She couldn't do that to Gabe. He still clung to it.

She turned it over in her hands. It was worn. The cards were worn. Tony had insisted they were valuable beyond number. Worn baseball cards. He had insisted Gabe carry it everywhere even when Gabe was too young to read.

"I'll try to fix it. Let's see what we can do to help save the cards. Come on."

Inside, they worked on repairing and fastening the cards together. Gabe babbled about fishing, Jason, shells, baseball and Maine wildlife. Always such a quiet, withdrawn child, she was amazed at his knowledge and interests. Moving to Trenton was a beneficial one for her son.

Talking himself to exhaustion, Gabe fell asleep on the table with his dinner before him, his book of cards in his lap. Marlo carried him to bed, placing the precious cards on the shelf next to his head. Maybe if the cards were the only thing he remembered of Tony as he grew that wouldn't be a bad thing.

She didn't want him to grow up without a father image in his head. No father.

She slumped on the chair nearest the porch and watched the sunset and darkness overtake her house. She listlessly sat. Cooking and baking didn't appeal to her. Brent had sparked a new interest in life. When he left, she felt the void.

A sharp rap on the door startled her and broke the reverie. Darkness enveloped the outside. Who knocked at nine o'clock? Wishing she had a dog for protection, she attempted to sound brave. "What?" she said. "Who is it? What do you want?"

"It's Brent. Marlo, I know it's late, but I just had to talk."

She flung open the door. "What's wrong? Are you okay?" He stepped inside, but moved no further.

"I needed to see you. I just got back. I came here. A cup of coffee would be good, if you don't mind, and can I come in?"

He looked disheveled and tired. Lines in his face emphasized the strain and made his eyes seem flat, not their usual blazing blue.

"Come in." With her hand on his arm, she directed him to the stool next to the center aisle in the kitchen. The dimmed lights created warmth in the room. She immediately prepared coffee and absentmindedly cut a generous piece of apple pie and placed it before him.

He smiled. "You always have something to make one feel at home." He held her hand. "Marlo, I've thought about you all week. I know I left in a hurry with only a message. I should have called or said something. I've never felt this way."

The awkwardness of his jumbled garble and the intensity of his gaze created an overwhelming need to be close to him. He gazed her palm with his thumb. She stepped closer.

"Brent, you're back." Gabe stumbled out to the kitchen and struggled into Brent's lap. "We have to fish. I caught a ten-inch with Jason. Mom and I fixed my baseball cards. I'll show you."

She watched Brent's interaction with her son. She had missed him more than she wanted to admit. She couldn't give him up, or live here without contact with him. He was a special man in both their lives. And he was here, he had come home.

"Come on, young man, back to bed." She held Gabe's hand

and led him to bed. "You can talk tomorrow when you and Brent are not so tired."

Brent walked to a deck chair in the middle of the deck. The soft murmur of the incoming waves was comforting. While on stakeout sitting in a beat-up vehicle on Portland streets, images of Marlo filled his thoughts. Although her secrecy, her nervousness indicated a troubled woman who guarded secrets. But her interactions with Gabe, his family and him indicated a trustworthy, unselfish woman. He'd bet his badge, her anxiety about her past was not about something she had done. As a police chief, he trusted instincts and everything in him said she was worthy of pursuit.

He rubbed his palm along the smooth wood of the arm of Adirondack chair. Whatever her hesitations, he'd wait until she felt ready to share her secrets. He wanted her in his life … He wanted more than that.

He rose when Marlo appeared at the porch sliding door.

"You didn't get to finish your pie. Your coffee is ready." She held out her hand which Brent took and followed her to the kitchen.

He perched on the stool as she set a cup of coffee and sugar and cream on the center aisle. "I'm glad you're back."

His easy smile caught her off-guard. "I thought of you while I was away."

Every time his gaze her hers, her heart turned over in response. In her confusion, the cream pitcher slipped from her fingers. She mopped the spill and kept her eyes averted.

His hand covered hers. "You were in my thoughts for many things. A problem haunts you." When she startled in response, he kept his hand firmly on top of hers. "A terror you are unwilling to share."

Marlo released her hand and refilled the pitcher near the refrigerator. She paused and didn't return to his side. "There are things in my life I need to settle before …" She pushed her hair behind her left eye. "Before I can think of another person in my life," she quickly finished.

He stood. "That's one of the things I've thought of. I still want to see you. I am willing to wait until you trust me enough to share your problems." He stepped beside her. "If you want to continue together."

She bit her bottom lip. She wanted to see Brent, but she would never be able to tell him of her past. She wanted a normal life. She wanted to appear normal. That was a lie. She wanted to be closer to Brent. She'd missed him while he was gone. She liked the time she spent with him. She would just have to be careful, careful enough to trust him with details of whom and what she was.

She raised her eye. "I like being with you." Her voice was soft. "I was afraid when you left such a curt message and didn't call, you didn't want to see me."

He gathered her into his arms and held her snugly against him. "I should have contacted you. I work for other forces in the state occasionally. I'm sorry I just left a message." His head rested on top of hers. He didn't want to let go. "I need to go home. I haven't slept much in the last week. I just couldn't wait another day to see you." She snuggled closer to his chest. If he stayed much longer and she moved any closer, he would want more and he didn't want to move too quickly.

He leaned down and kissed her. One goodnight kiss was not enough. He kissed her again. He liked the taste of her lips like wild berries growing only in Maine. His fingers caressed the back of her head and tangled in the softness of her hair. A soft sound from her lips encouraged him and he sucked her bottom lip in and tantalized it with his tongue. Her hands gripped his arms. He needed to go home before his instincts took over and he flipped her onto the nearby couch and tasted more than her lips. "Good night, Marlo," he whispered. "Sweet dreams." He kissed her once more and left.

Marlo's palms on the closed door held her steady. She felt as if she could fly and danced across the ceiling. *So that's what kisses could do to you.* No one had ever made her feel that way.

She checked in on Gabe. His regular breathing sounded reassuring. The move to Maine had helped them both. Maybe if she developed acting skills and hid her past, they could share a good life here. Miriam had helped her develop Marlo Saunders, maybe she could help her invent a past life. Miriam had instructed her to keep a low profile and keep on the lookout for a year. Could she invent a self that Brent would accept? She'd have to be careful. Before she could get back to her bed, the phone rang.

"Hi, thanks for letting me in. I needed to see you," Brent said.

She smiled and cuddled the phone against her cheek.

"Tomorrow night, a second date. Ways to get to know each other."

She nodded. *I am free to date. It can't harm my cover and no one is around to tell me no.* "Yes, a second date." The words came out slowly and deliberately.

"Second date, we'll go dancing."

"Dancing?" Images of old grainy musicals and vintage Bandstand flashed before her eyes. What dancing did people do now? "Dancing?"

"Yep, that's the appropriate second date. It's the excuse to clutch each other close." She heard the laughter in his voice, he continued. "As teens, it fooled our moms into thinking we were good. We could cling close, rubbing bodies."

She laughed just picturing Brent as a teen. "Were you the one mothers had to warn their daughters about?"

His deep laugh warmed her even through the phone. She could make him laugh. What a wonderful feeling. Dancing? She hadn't danced since high school. She had loved Friday nights in the gym gyrating to the latest tunes. Her Aunt Mabel had hated it and discouraged her interest as too sensual and inviting for teens. "I am not a good dancer."

"Neither are most of my siblings. When you're dancing close, *real* close, finesse doesn't matter."

If he were in front of her, she would see his blue eyes and infectious grin.

"I want to be near you." His voice changed to a husky low tone. "Dancing assures we can be close."

"Oh? And do I have to worry about you on the dance floor?"

"Dancing assures we can be close, but you're safe with my siblings and mother as witnesses."

"Your mother?"

"You don't have to dance with her."

His laugh, the one that seemed to start deep within, echoed

though the phone. Every time Marlo heard that laugh, it made her grin and feel good. "Ok, so I don't have to dance with your mother, but she is on our date?" Teasing and flirting were new skills. "Your siblings, do I dance with them?"

Again she elicited a laugh. "Welcome to Trenton. Every Friday there's a dance night. All types of music for every age. It's the drawstring that pulls together generations in town. All my siblings will be there. Gabe comes, too, on this date. No baby sitters. No worries. Except dancing close in front of the whole family. Are you ready?"

She paused. She wanted to blend into the town, but dancing in front of people? She would be with Brent and be in the secure sensuous fold his arms. She plopped on the nearby couch. "Sure, I'm ready."

"Pick you up at seven. Night. Sweet dreams."

Marlo rocked back and forth on the couch hugging her knees. A date. A dance. Life was so good. Feeling younger than she had in years, she fell asleep with a smile.

Awakened by a shrill ring, she grabbed the phone crashing off the couch. "Are you in bed, Marlene Defalco?" A husky voice shot her wide awake her heart pounding. A shape click followed. She sat up, her back against the bed staring at the phone on her lap. Someone knew her. Knew her name. Knew her number.

She awoke the next morning curled on the floor, the phone flopped haphazardly across her arm. She placed the phone on the table and watched it. Did she get that call last night or were her fears now interrupting her thoughts?

Tonight she and Gabe had exciting plans. She didn't want her old life interfering. She stumbled to the kitchen and prepared coffee. Did someone call? Or was she dreaming?

She sat on the deck facing the water sipping her morning coffee. No boats. No calls. She looked out as streaks of morning sun glowed along her shoreline. Fears of her past choked the small joys she had. She needed to trust herself and to trust Brent. To let go of the nightmares of her past and become the person she wanted to be.

Gabe dragged a pair of pants behind him. He climbed onto her lap. He snuggled up next to her. "Mommy, my jeans have holes." He laid his jeans on her knee. She fingered the holes. Gabe's first jeans. Tony had never let him wear jeans. His first jeans showed signs of play. Happy signs.

"You're right, Gabe. We need clothes for tonight. We're going to a dance with friends. Come on!"

She bought a short pleated skirt and a matching vest. Reveling in her freedom to buy clothes and anticipating an exciting night, she sang as she dressed that evening. The vest clung to her figure in all the right places. Her skirt fell above her knee. She laughed. She could even relish feeling good about the person in the mirror. Gabe, dressed in new jeans and eager for the dinner and movie provided for children, made her leave early.

Marlo hesitated at the doorway. Nothing looked familiar. People were moving to a beat alien to her day and memories. Standing on the sideline, she watched bodies wiggle, stomp, turn and dip. Caught up in the music and the tempo of the evening, Marlo tapped her foot and hummed.

"Come on." Alisha and two sisters and several nieces dragged her with them to the floor. So many O'Neills. Marlo didn't know most of their names. What now? "Twist Again" blared from the speaker. She couldn't hold back the chuckle, even she knew this.

Forming a circle in the middle of the floor, the O'Neill crew led the party in twisting. Marlo shrugged her shoulders and experimented moving her hips.

"Come on! " Alisha yelled from across the circle. "Loosen up. No one cares what you look like. Or your dancing ability." Marlo tossed back her hair, tilted back her head and flung herself into the sounds and beat of the music. Laughing aloud at the circular contortions, she relaxed and spun to the beat. The song's end was a disappointment.

Before she could catch her breath, a male touched her shoulder. "Hi, I'm Cal Hooven. You've seen me at the hardware store. Care to dance?"

The evening was more than she anticipated. Each dance she had a new partner. She learned steps to a new beat and met many new faces from town.

"This is the part I like best." Brent appeared at her side

and clasped his arms around her waist. "And this is where I turn away any other Trenton's males. They won't cut in on the police chief. I didn't think I was ever going to get a turn." With the first note of the slow number, Brent moved closer so their bodies swayed together in a sultry move with each step. "You looked pretty sexy there swinging those hips around."

"I did?"

"Sure, couldn't wait for a slow number so I could swing those hips next to me." Each step they took, his body edged closer. "This is why I've always liked these dances. Get scandalously close right before everyone's eyes." His arms closed around her waist bringing her to a tighter embrace. His muscles caressed all of her as he swung her around the floor. The music ended. She was only inches from his face. She held her breath, closed her eyes, expecting his kiss, wanting his kiss.

Running his fingers down her arm, he reached for her hand. "Come on. Line dance." He wasn't going to kiss her, that distressed her. He nodded toward the floor where all his family stood looking at them.

"Family line dance time."

"I can't do this. I don't know how."

"I'm going to teach you." He shifted her behind Alisha. "Follow her." Brent with his hands on her hips maneuvered her to the left. As the music filled the hall, his hands guided her body in the correct direction. Alisha followed a routine seemingly known by everyone else. Marlo followed Alisha.

Laughter erupted when she shifted left and the entire family moved right and she ran into Alisha. Brent's hands spun her to the right or left and he pushed her forward as the dance progressed. Marlo leaned back into his body letting his warmth encircle her. They moved as one. As the beat increased, his arms crossed in front of her chest, his palms rested on her hips as they danced as one. The touch of his hardened muscles along the length of her body was intoxicating. Marlo lost her sense of time and place and felt only the movement of their bodies.

Her hair fell in front of her face, beads of perspiration formed on her upper lip. Her body ached from exertion, but it felt good. This was not the dream world described in books, but real people enjoying life and she could share it. When the music stopped, she was breathless. A circle of siblings clapped and cheered. "Good start. Wait until the next one."

"Oh my God." Marlo pointed to the O'Neill faces in front of her. "Alisha, Brent, Cameron, Dana, Ericka and Frank. What was your mother thinking?"

"I don't know that thinking was what started six kids," Alisha quipped.

"No, your names, alphabetical? The O'Neill alphabet?"

"Them's fighting words. We've beaten many a child for that." A circle of bodies moved closer. With no perceptible signal, they put hands on her and lifted her high above the heads on the dance floor. "Say uncle and apologize for the family insult."

Giggles pealed from her lips. "Apologize for the truth?" The hands tossed her high and caught her.

"Okay, okay, *uncle!*" They dropped her directly into Brent's arms. The security and tension in his arms caused an unexpected warmth to surge through her body.

She slid down to her own feet, her hands still rested on Brent's shoulders. "I've never done anything like that. Your family is crazy. Are they always this way?"

Brent glanced at the cluster huddled neat the punch bowl. "Ohh yes. They've always been crazy. It's a family trait."

"Lucky to have so many to be a part of your life. I'll be back. I'm going to check on Gabe." When Marlo returned, she interrupted a heated discussion among the brothers and sisters.

"Fourth Of July?" Marlo asked Alisha. A hush enveloped the group. "What did I interrupt?"

"The cottage is the place for the family Fourth of July picnic each year. Fireworks are out over the water." Cameron moved from the main group and confronted her. "They don't want to ask your permission to use the cottage."

Cameron stood directly in front of her separating her from the family. Brent, still in the other room, was not there to provide support.

"I certainly won't stand in the way. I'm only staying there." She began weakly. "You shouldn't give up ... family is important."

"You don't have to do this." Brent walked to her side.

"No, Brent, please, I can help."

Alisha rescued her by chiming in. "She loves to bake, Brent. She would be a great addition to the picnic." Alisha crowded both her brothers out of the way. "It's a great tradition. Fireworks. Fishing races in the morning. Those who like to, cook. Those who like baking, do so. Those who want to fish or just loaf, do so. It's an all-day affair."

Marlo chewed on the corner of her lip. All of the O'Neill including recalcitrant Cameron at her place? A sense of foreboding tightened a knot in her stomach. She couldn't shut out his family. They had been good to her. "Sounds like fun. You tell me what you need. I'll clean the house."

"Don't bother," Dana, his sister, said. "All of us tramping through, it's not worth it to clean anything." She turned to her brother. "Except the grills. We need them and you can do that."

"You sure you're up to this?" Brent asked.

"I'd love to." Marlo directed her response to Brent. "Everyone has welcomed me, made me feel apart of activities, even taught me dances." She looked at Cameron over Brent's shoulder. The scowl on Cameron's face showed his displeasure, even now. What had she done to him? Did he know about Tony? Would she ever escape the dark cloud over her head? The group was silent watching her. She redirected their attention by stating, "Tell me about the day and what help you think will be appropriate."

Alisha linked her arm in Marlo's and whispered, "Good recovery. My family likes you already."

Alisha said to Brent, "I think you should be in charge of all desserts. Think of her last desserts you tasted. We would think up an event just to get her to make more desserts."

"M-m-m, I do remember those." Gone from Brent's eyes was the anxiety, the compelling blue gaze returned. He held her spellbound just with his eyes. "You promised lots of desserts if I was a good boy. I'll just have to prove how good I am."

His statement brought murmured response from the men behind him. Brent turned to his brothers. "I meant on the dance floor, Neanderthals. Which is where we're going so you don't eavesdrop. Come on." He slipped his arm around her and easily moved her away from Alisha. On the dance floor, he said. "As I mentioned, my family is overbearing."

"They're wonderful." Marlo couldn't hide her enthusiasm. "I really am looking forward to it. Gabe has never seen fireworks."

"When was the last time you saw fireworks?"

Marlo swallowed back tears long buried. A Fourth of July celebration with her parents and Emerson seventeen years ago came to mind. She had forced those memories to the back of her mind. "A very long time ago," she said softly.

Brent rubbed her back, his fingers threaded a path up the bones of her spine. "You missed much in your life. Time to make up for that." He deftly swung her around in time to the country beat. "For you, not just for Gabe. You'll like the fireworks and the celebration."

"It's been a long time since I celebrated much in my life." She stretched up so she could wrap her arms around his neck as another slow song played. His fingers moving along her back felt so rewarding. She could lose herself in this man's arms, let him take away her burdens.

He danced closer to the edge of the floor and when the music stopped, they were sheltered behind a potted plant and a curtain. He leaned into her and kissed her. A shiver of desire ran through her. She wanted him in a way she had never desired Tony.

She slowly ran her tongue along his upper lip. He tasted like cola. She experimented with laving the inside of his lip. Brent covered her mouth with his and his kiss this time was hard and demanding. Her breath came faster. She matched his exploration with his tongue. A brush fire blaze started at the tip of her head and swept rapidly throughout her body. His arms wrapped around her and pulled her tight against him.

"Uncle Brent, Mommy says we're doing the family last dance. You're supposed to come in. You, too." Terry, a niece announced. Both jumped apart. Marlo rubbed her hand across her lips and smoothed down her hair. She attempted to calm her racing heart and her overheated body before she faced his siblings.

"Soon. We'll have time to ourselves, I promise," Brent said.

Returning home late, she tucked a tired Gabe in his bed. The low lights cast a warm glow in the cottage and mirrored the warm glow inside. The feeling of Brent's strong arms encircling her; the desire he stirred within her created restlessness.

The past is past. A new life initiated here in Maine. Tony was gone. Gabe had friends. Her interest in Brent bloomed.

She gave Gabe one final pat. *We're okay, Gabe. We're going to be fine, healthy.* She smiled. *We're going to celebrate the nation's birth. We're going to have a life with friends, parties and people in our lives. And Brent in our life.*

She shut the door.

Chapter Five

When the phone rang, Gabe and Marlo stared at it. Twice it had rung in the past three days. Each time, Marlo's heart stopped, but each time the person hung up. It rang again. She paused, then answered.

"Doing any baking over there? I've been thinking about that mousse you made the other day." Brent's voice resounded. Her fingers loosened their death grip on the receiver. Had he called twice and not hearing her "hello," hung up?

"I have been thinking about what I'll make for the Fourth of July. Maybe, I'll try some experiments and you can sample."

"My family is quite a crew at one time. Are you sure you want the Fourth of July there? My mom's house would hold everyone and we could drive to a spot to see the fireworks."

"No." Marlo said firmly. "We've discussed this. It's your family tradition and I am merely staying until your cousin comes."

"If you are sure. I need to get a couple of things ready. Is it okay if I come over late afternoon today? I'll gladly sample any dessert experiments you might have."

Marlo's pulse quickened. She and Brent would work together before the holiday, which was another advantage to agreeing to the picnic. "We'll be here. I'd like to help, too. You could have just come over, Brent."

"You have a life. Don't want to intrude on any plans you might have. You've met many in Trenton, some at the dance yesterday."

"I'm not interested in any. My only friends are your family. If you come over within an hour, I'll fix you lunch." She leaned over and handed Gabe a piece of tape to fix his ever present baseball card collection.

"I get off at one. I'll come right over if you have lunch then."

"Agreed."

Gabe latched onto Brent before he entered the door. Gabe chattered about fishing, friends and baseball cards as Brent reached for the cup of coffee Marlo offered. Brent sat at the seat Marlo indicated and Gabe jumped into his lap showing off his possessions.

"My dad gave me this collection." Gabe flipped through the plastic pages showing off the brightly colored clips of baseball heroes.

"I don't know much about cards. My brothers were avid collectors. They'd be impressed." A father. When did Gabe see him? Marlo avoided talking about him and flinched when Gabe had just mentioned him. Maybe mentioning the father when just he and Gabe were together would give him some answers.

As Marlo handed Brent his lunch, Gabe scrambled off and outside. "Does your family dance like that every time they're together? This morning, my body felt like I had been dancing all night."

Brent swallowed his sandwich bite whole. He had been imagining that body all morning and the feel of her swinging hips beneath his hands as they twirled down the line.

"You're a natural. You perfected all the steps."

"Only with your hands on my hips did I move in the right direction."

He winked. "That's the idea. I had my hands on you."

Marlo picked up the plates and moved to the sink. What had she thought of yesterday's dancing. Did she move away because she didn't want his touches or because she was flustered by his comments and wanted more?

"Let's take coffee on the deck and then you can point out my jobs for the day," she said.

The jobs he had in mind were sinking into his arms and losing themselves in kisses and touching and … He sighed and took the cup from her hand. He needed to learn to keep his mind on the task at hand and not let thoughts of her misdirect him.

Marlo leaned against the railing, her mug halfway to her mouth. "Your second date was a success. What's the next?" Her smile and the merriment in her eyes surprised him. Finally, a breakthrough. She teased back.

"Hmm." He menacingly moved closer. "So you admit it. You like me and you want more dates." Before she could react, he pulled her into his arms and kissed her nose, each cheek, then trailed a series of kisses down her throat. Marlo folded in half in his arms and peals of laughter shook her frame. He tickled her throat again with her to him, slamming her into his chest. Thoughts of holding her had disturbed him all day. "I have plans for the next date."

She said nothing. He felt her shallow breathing next to his chest. "Do I scare you?'

She leaned back facing him. She took a deep breath, a tentative smile followed. "When do I get to plan the dates?"

"You admitted it. More dates even after the third date."

"We'll see what happens on this date. Movies and dancing have been good—wonderful." Her fingers touched his shoulder and moved across his shirt to his collar opening. Brent reveled in her initiated touch. She wasn't immune to his interest and she reciprocated. Throwing her across his shoulder and carting her off to a private spot would answer his urges. He'd have to take care with her; something or someone in her past had made her very frightened of touches, and intimacy.

He tangled his fingers in the softness of her auburn curls. "The next date will be special. Knock-you-off-your-feet special. Then if you don't like it you plan the rest of our dates."

Marlo's heart pounded against her ribs. The next dates. Brent obviously didn't want this to end any more than she did. Both dates had left her breathless and eager with anticipation for the next time. Brent left her breathless and eager with or without the dates.

His finger tickled the side of her face. "When do you want this … next date."

His smoldering eyes created blanks in her thinking. Next? Now? "Now we are supposed to be getting ready for a family picnic. The next will have to wait until after the Fourth."

He moved back. "You're right. I have grills to clean and benches to move. But while I'm doing that I'll be thinking of the next date."

Her smile had an air of devilish charm. "I'll work right next to you so you will think of nothing else." Working next to him, sharing time with him would be the best date she could think of right now. His mere presence was enough.

"Look!" Brent held her hand and pointed to the sky. "Watch the peregrine falcon. That was a rare bird on the endangered list. Watch him dive for food." With utmost precision, the bird dashed deep into the sea.

She studied Brent's face as he watched. The man was delightful puzzle. So much of him she didn't know. He loved this area. His tales of wild life and ocean were part of him. So much delight in learning the many facets of him.

Marlo worked beside Brent scrubbing layers of ash from four grills. "We will use all of these?" With back of her wrist, she moved her hair from her eyes.

"My family? It's big and they eat."

"So what happens here on the Fourth?"

"Games, friendly competition, food and fireworks." Brent dismantled the grill. "In the morning, parent-child groupings have a fishing contest." He reached for the cloth in his back pocket. "If you think he'd like it, I'll take Gabe as my partner. I've never had one."

Marlo stopped scrubbing. Brent as Gabe's parent? Did Brent realize the significance of what he had said? Brent would be the best thing in Gabe's life. A real parent with good values, not a crook.

Brent looked up. "I think Gabe would like it. I couldn't replace his real father. He obviously has some attachment there."

Marlo flushed. She didn't like the tone of the conversation. "He loves time with you. He loves fishing. I'm sure he would agree to the contest." She vigorously scrubbed with a brush.

"Gabe must miss his father."

The line hung in the air as if Brent had waved a sword between them. Marlo continued scrubbing, her hands trembling. "The father is away. We don't talk about it much.

He doesn't like to," she quickly added, fearful Brent might ask questions of Gabe.

"You don't talk about him much." Brent had stopped his cleaning.

"No." She focused on a dirty clump, then rapidly obliterated it.

His hand covered hers stopping the movement. "Where is he?"

"Gone. He's not coming here."

"We're getting close. Dating. You're not still involved with him? He's not going to storm in here looking for you, is he?"

Marlo felt as if a blanket had covered her face. Her breathing was labored. Him showing up here looking for her was an impossibility. Miriam had promised that Marlo was safe and Tony was behind bars. Tony would never look in Maine. What did Brent know? How close was he to knowing her greatest fear? She had to play this carefully. "He won't come here. He's not in my life."

"Are you going to tell me about him?" Brent had gripped her wrist and turned her to him.

"No." Marlo forced herself to keep steady and to look directly into his eyes. "No, it's none of your concern."

Brent ground his teeth. She wouldn't let down. Who was this man for her to protect him? Did she still love her ex? Was he a fool for becoming interested in Marlo? Her stance stiff, her eyes blank stare made her seem determined and tough. Her chin gave her away—the quiver clued him to her faked resolve. He stroked the outside of her arm. "Relax, Marlo, I won't pressure you where you don't want to go. Not on anything. I will learn more." The last line was more to himself.

He should find out about her. His reluctance to do so was unhealthy for a policeman and owner of this property. She returned to erasing dirt on the grill with no response to him. He worked quietly. A shudder in her shoulders caught his attention. Had he made her cry? Were thoughts of her husband that bad?

He wrapped his arms around the front of her and leaned her back on him. "Quiet, dear Marlo. It's not worth crying about." A sniffle revealed he was right. "We're friends with or without your past. We have much to do today. I don't want you crying and not working. I don't want to upset you so you can't make all those desserts I'm dreaming of for the Fourth."

His last line hit the mark, he felt the tension leave her body. He kissed the back of her head, then returned to his own space. "What desserts are you making for the Fourth?"

"How many do you think I should make?" She wiped her nose with tissue, reached for her cleaning cloth.

"As many as you can. I'd like to sample them all."

She faced him. "I can create a kitchen full, if desserts are your weakness. What else can I do?"

"That will be plenty." The safe topic eased the tension between them. "Cameron doesn't fish with his daughter, Nancy does. He barbecues and smokes the main course while we fish. Everyone brings something to eat. My sister coordinates that. You have your assignment: desserts!"

As they cleaned Brent didn't mention Tony again, but the quiet barrier between them remained. Marlo withdrew into a shell.

Brent hoped the Fourth and sharing the crazy day with him would break down another barrier she had erected. Getting her to tease, to laugh, even to admit she liked something had been a step. With help of his family's antics, he would get close again.

Marlo anticipated the excitement of a holiday. She baked for two days. The fishermen and their partners arrived early. Gabe, anxious to be a fishing partner, awoke at five AM.

The cottage was full of noise, challenges, and banter as the partners organized. After the fishing parties departed, Marlo was left with a stone quiet cottage and Cameron. Cameron said nothing to her in the morning and stationing himself outside, stoked the fires on the huge grills. Marlo tried not to look up at Cameron as he worked just outside the window of the deck. His frowning physique at each family gathering was enough to ward her away. She arranged the fancy desserts and baked the last batches of cookies for the day.

So engrossed in her task, she didn't hear Cameron until he was in the kitchen. Cameron leaned against the end of the cupboard. Marlo waited. Cameron's stance, his arms crossed, his lips tightly pursed, revealed he was sizing her up. She kept filling cookie trays with diagonal slices of raspberry slings. The kitchen's aroma of cinnamon and freshly baked dough seemingly had no effect on Cameron.

"Why did you come to Maine?" His pose didn't change.

Marlo concentrated on the food. She hadn't thought of an answer for that. Certainly the real reason, it was chosen for her, would lead to other questions she didn't dare answer.

"I like the isolation. I hated big cities with the anonymity. I know this is a safe place for Gabe to grow up."

"You're a city girl, seems odd you would settle for such a vast difference in lifestyles in one move." He didn't state he thought she was liar, but Marlo felt the accusation.

Cameron reached for a warm cookie from the nearest platter and nibbled on the edge. His eyes never moved from his scrutiny of her face. "What made you latch on to my brother?"

Marlo met his gaze. "Brent talked to us. He went out of his way to be nice. I'm indebted to your brother for helping us settle here."

"You can't hide behind my brother's good nature. Some people pick up stray pups. Brent picks up stray people. He can't help reaching out to those undeserving weaklings who are hiding and need a good man to solve their problems."

Marlo winced at the accurate jabs. She placed the last slice on the platter and moved toward Cameron. "I'm not living off your brother. I'm not destitute or homeless."

"You didn't deny you were hiding. What's your rent?"

Nothing wasn't an answer she wanted to give. Brent hadn't charged them anything so far. "That's between Brent and me. I'm not about to reveal his financial arrangements."

Cameron snorted. "We're not a secretive family. Just what have you done to mesmerize my brother so he doesn't see the flaws you are covering."

"Just what flaws?"

"The fact that none of us knows anything about you: your age, previous address, previous record, martial status. On computer, you don't exist."

Marlo bit her lip to hold back the gasp. If Brent looked,

what could he find? If Cameron could look for things, how easy would it be for others to find her?

"I see that concerns you." Cameron continued, "I'll make sure Brent uses every source available to dig out your past. He was devastated once by a lying, deceitful woman. I won't let it happen again." After his parting shot, Cameron returned to the barbecue grills.

Marlo stared out the window. What connections did Brent have? As police chief, he should be investigating her. What had he found? Yet, he trusted her. He rented this place without knowing her. Was she a stray dog to him, an available stray dog who melted at his kisses? Certainly, she hadn't discouraged his advances. His kisses set her heart on fire.

Marlo checked the last two trays of cookies. She cherished the time she had spent with Brent. She loved. Love? She burnt her hand on the cookie trays, sending cookies sliding across the floor. Love? Would she know what love was?

She flopped on the nearest chair with ice cubes wrapped in a towel against the red welt on her fingers. She had meandered into a destructive relationship with Tony to escape the confines of her aunt's household. Tony seemed the perfect man. Suave, learned, fancy. He bought the best in clothes for her and for him, but she was a mere ornament on his arm. Later his flaws shone through, but she was too young, too demure to do anything.

Now, she coped with carving her own life. She was learning to be strong, decisive. Love now in her life? She had too much to learn about life before she would be misled by the kindness of another man. Certainly, other women in town held more attractions for Brent. She tossed her towel in the sink and scooped up a pile of cookies.

She couldn't stay. If Brent investigated her and opened files on her, others could, too. If Brent discovered her past, she certainly wouldn't be welcome here. Surely in the vast United States, other isolated towns existed. If Brent's family distrusted her as much as Cameron, she needed to leave. Brent's family meant the world to him. She couldn't interfere in that. She couldn't hurt him. She couldn't have a normal life here. Her life with Tony had assured that. She couldn't let her need for friends or the desires Brent elicited cloud her vision. She had her evil past to hide. Discovery could destroy her son.

Marlo heard Gabe's laughter and chatter from down below. Gabe loved it here, but they needed to move on. Gabe and Brent simultaneously raced in the door.

"Smells wonderful in here." Brent surveyed the display of twenty dozen cookies behind her. He walked behind her, glancing over her shoulder at the cookies she decorated. Reaching around her, his arm brushing her breast as he moved, he grabbed a cookie. He remained behind her, toying with her curls while he munched on a cookie.

"What happened here?" Brent pointed to the cookies scattered on the floor. "Look at your hand. You okay baking all these cookies?"

"Mommy bakes great." Gabe grabbed a few of the cooling cookies. "Daddy never ate any, but that meant more for me."

Silence dominated the room. Marlo felt Brent's hand tighten on the shoulder. She grabbed a broom and frantically swept the crumbs from the floor. Brent bent and held a dust pan.

Gabe, with cookie midway to his mouth, cried, "Oh, Mommy, I'm sorry. I didn't mean to talk about Daddy."

Marlo handed Brent a heavily laden plate of decorated cookies. "Please take these out to a table."

She bent down in front of Gabe. "It's okay. An honest slip is okay. How was fishing?" Unwilling to upset Gabe and bring out more comments, she turned his focus.

By the time Brent returned, Gabe was in the middle of his story. "And the big one I caught, it was this big." Gabe stretched his arms out. "Got away. I really fought to catch him, but I almost had him on board when he slipped."

Marlo couldn't help but smile at Gabe's enthusiastic tale.

"He'll be a real fisherman, yet." Brent slipped his arms around Gabe shoulders. "Telling stories of the one that got away is a sure sign of a great fisherman."

Gabe looked up at Brent. Marlo noted the hero worship in Gabe's expression. It would be difficult to take Gabe away from him. "We did come in third." Gabe wrapped in arms around Brent's like they were buddies. "Third in the parent-child contest. Brent caught one, too."

The sight of Gabe and Brent arm in arm brought a lump to Marlo's throat. Brent, dark hair disheveled, his jeans smudged with dirt, had a potent magnetism. Marlo stopped herself from running her fingers through that hair and touching him with the same ardor her son showed. Brent would be difficult man to leave.

She couldn't afford to get any more attached, she had to distance herself. Now! She had let down her guard and become too close. Her emotions couldn't be love, simply lust.

The warm smile he showered on her and Gabe was irresistible. She touched his arm. "Brent, thank you for all you have done for us. Thank you for the day you have given Gabe." His warmth and viable spirit ran from her fingertips straight to her heart. She couldn't become attached to this man. "I'm taking all this outside."

Avoiding Brent was difficult, wherever she turned he was there. His hand accidentally touched her hand, her back, her arm, each move she made. Each touch sent shivers of regret. She sought solace in the kitchen away from the food and family.

Brent followed and confronted her. "Why are you avoiding me?"

"I'm not." She reached for the box of trash bags. "I'm starting to clean up."

"Yes, you are." He tilted her chin. The full force of his bright blues eyes caused her heart to flutter. She fought the attraction his mere presence.

"You slip away and you haven't said three words to me all afternoon. What's bothering you?"

"Nothing. I'm busy with desserts."

"You can't avoid me in the games. You're my partner."

"What games?" She dropped the box on the floor. No one said games and partners.

"Come on." He hooked his finger in hers and took her to Gabe. "Gabe, what comes next?"

"Mommy, I'm going to be in the sack race. If I win, I get my pick of candy prizes." Gabe pointed to the gang of children and adults gathering on the neighbor's field. "Mommy, what's a sack race? There's other races I can win. I've never done this.

Next year, I'll win with the biggest fish." All his sentences ran into one. His hair was messy, his face red.

Marlo tugged a piece of dirt from his hair. Gone was the silent, watchful child. She needed to protect him from his past, but she needed to let him enjoy his present. Brent laced his fingers inside hers and leaned his hip against her. She couldn't pull away, nor did she want to.

"Mrs. Carlson joins us for the Fourth and we use her field for a day for friendly competitions. All participate." He poked her in the arm. "You, too." Brent turned to Gabe. "Come on, let's go find you a sack and I'll explain the finer rules."

"Come on, Mom, this is the bestest day ever. You play, too." He ran after Brent.

Alisha tapped her on the shoulder and motioned her to the side. "We need your help in the tug of war."

"You'd better fill in the whole story," added Nancy, Cameron's wife. "We women lose every year. One more body may help. We're tired of getting wet."

Marlo frowned. "If you always lose, why play? And how do you get wet in a tug of war?"

"It's on Mrs. Carlson's bridge. It connects her land to the forest across a side section of the bay. The guys always drag us into the water. And we do it because it's the Fourth and we … always do. Cameron provides the anchor; he's on the end with the rope around his waist. He's tough," Nancy filled in.

"What is that awful gleam in your eye?" Alisha glanced at Marlo. "I've not seen that look. What?"

Marlo whispered to the others and peels of laughter brought the attention of the men.

"Okay, I'll get the rest of the women. You go watch Gabe," Alisha said.

Brent met Marlo on the side to the field. "He's going to fall. Don't embarrass him by running over to pick him up."

"Why would I do that?"

Brent pulled up a piece of Timothy grass and stuck it between his teeth. "Gabe gave me directions. He's afraid you'll embarrass him."

"He said that?"

Brent nodded. "He loves you, Mom, but he needs to take a

few falls."

Marlo kept silent. Gabe had enough tragedies in his life. Brent squeezed her fingers and pointed. Gabe, so eager, had tumbled over at the starting line. She smiled and glanced at Brent who winked. After falling two or three times, Gabe did finish.

Brent held up a package of candy with a flourish, he patted it into Gabe's hand. "For a real competitor and my fishing partner. Now let's see how well your mom and I do."

Marlo watched other adults at the starting line. "We're doing what?"

Brent leaned into her. "Three-legged race. You keep your leg and hips tight against mine. I hold onto your waist and don't let you fall." He fastened a soft rope around their ankles. She felt the rope dig through her sock. The greatest concern would be the closeness of Brent's body. Longing warmed her more than the July heat.

Brent's hand rested on her hip. His fingers drew circles.

"We need to synchronize our steps or we fall on each other." Brent's eyes glimmered with a mischievous look. "You'll break my fall if I fall on top. If we win, we kiss in celebration. If we lose, we kiss so we don't feel bad."

Marlo giggled. Brent's ability to bring out that laughter weakened her resolve to distance herself.

"Good ploy, huh? I hold you close." He tightened his hold on her waist. "And kiss you." The whistle blew. Marlo's outer leg barely touched the ground as Brent carried her. They crossed the finish line and landed in a heap of bodies.

"Tie, tie, tie," the judge pronounced and tapped Marlo's head.

"Come on." Brent pulled her up, kissed her. He rested Marlo on his hip and carted her to the starting line. Applause and chuckles among the audience followed them. At the starting line, he kissed her again, slowly lingering as if pulling their lips apart were torture.

"Better watch yourself," Cameron said.

Marlo jerked into position and away from Brent's corrupting kisses.

Brent said, "Make sure we beat Cameron and Nancy. They

won last year."

Marlo pushed off and clung to Brent as he leaped down the line. They landed in a pile at the finishing line behind the winners. Brent's lower body nestled into hers. He held himself up by his forearms.

"This is why you race. Most men hope to lose, so your team ends in a pile." He didn't get up, but trailed a line of kisses starting on her forehead to her hairline to her neck. She giggled helplessly and wiggled beneath him.

"I like you best when I get you to laugh." With one palm resting on the ground near each shoulder and his knees on either side of her legs, she was trapped. "Tell me what has been bothering you all day."

"I can't." She attempted to wiggle out from other him, but succeeded only in rubbing her chest against his chest and thrusting her hips dangerously into his pelvic bone.

"Don't move. We'll both be safer. You rub against me like that and my family will have more to watch. You're dangerous, woman." The blue eyed gaze was full of promise. "You can't ignore me forever."

Alisha shouted. "Tug-of-War. Participants to the walkway."

Marlo beat Brent to the group. Alisha and the women eagerly awaited her appearance. They huddled and Marlo elaborated on the plan.

"Come on, come on," one of the men yelled. "Strategies can't help. The sooner we do this, the sooner we win and the sooner you get wet."

Marlo wrapped the end of the rope around her waist with a dramatized gesture. She waved to Cameron.

"Marlo's too tiny to give you any advantage," Cameron shouted.

"Marlo is our advantage this year," Alisha answered. "Ready? One, two, three." The women leaned back struggling hard. The men just held the rope.

"Okay, guys, same as last year … and the year before." Cameron braced his legs and the men yanked on the rope. The women let go as Marlo tossed her end in the air. She smirked as Cameron was the first in the slimy water. It wasn't revenge, she tried to reassure herself, but she felt satisfaction watching him bob in the water.

"Oh my, we lost, didn't we?" Alisha stood with her hands on her hips surveying her relatives in the bay. "Better luck next time, men." She high-fived Marlo. "Nice job. Welcome to the family!"

"Don't count on it." A red-raced and very wet Cameron emerged first. "One point for your side, Marlo. A shallow victory." Cameron stomped off.

Seeing the stricken look on Marlo's face, Alisha patted her arm. "He's a poor loser. They usually win. Nancy, go talk to your husband about manners."

Marlo avoided Cameron and stayed with Gabe for the remaining hours. She positioned herself with Gabe between her legs awaiting the fireworks.

"Mommy, isn't this the bestest day of your life? Aren't you glad we moved here?" Gabe said.

"Yeah, Mom, aren't you glad you moved here?" Brent flopped on the grass behind her so that her back rested against his chest. His body formed an arch around her so he could talk with Gabe and she could feel the protective wall around her.

The first burst of multi-colored lights brought ahh's from the crowd and silenced conversation. Gabe leaped up and down on her lap. Marlo, excited as her son, gripped Brent's arm. When the last burst of red, white and blue lit up the sky, she and Gabe were on their feet cheering. Her hair limply hung around her cheeks. Her shirt had dots of mustard from Gabe's hot dog and cookie colored sprinkles still clung to her sleeve, but the day had been the "bestest day ever" just as her son had proclaimed. She would never regret her time here.

At the end of the evening, Brent carried an exhausted Gabe to his own room in the cottage. Brent loaded his family's cars with leftovers and Marlo wiped counters and covered cookies.

"Here." Brent handed her a glass of wine. "Let's sit out here." She sat in the chair furthest from Brent on the deck. Brent remained at the railing, sipping his wine.

"What's been bothering you all day?" His voice so low she could barely hear it. She stared at the red liquid in her glass, then swirled it around.

"Brent, I'm not the woman you think I am. You gave us this place without knowing much about me."

"Should I be arresting you? There are no warrants out on you."

She startled at his statement. "Have you investigated me? Cameron said you had sources you could learn everything about me."

He faced her. He set his drink on the railing. "Is that what this is about? You thought I looked into your private life? Is that what Cameron told you?"

"You could if you wanted, couldn't you? Cameron said …"

He placed a finger up to her lips. "Don't actually say what Cameron told you. I might be tempted to beat him into the ground as I did when we were teens."

"Cameron asked about my past. He thinks you're making a mistake. You let us have your cottage. I haven't told you much."

Brent pulled up the other chair close enough so their knees touched. "It bothers me you don't trust me to tell me who you are or what fears cause the shadows in your eyes." He cupped her face in his hands. "But you are the person I think you are. You are the woman with much love to give. Look how you are with Gabe. You have a passion for life. You've been here a few weeks and are eager to experience a new world here. Despite your fears, you reach out to others. You've touched my family's life with kindness and caring. You are the person I think you are and I'm attracted to that woman."

Marlo let the words sink in. A glow flowed through her from his description. She wished she were that person.

"And you are attracted to me. Your body gives you away." His thumbs grazed her cheeks. "And you like this as well." His kiss was persuasive.

"You can't ask more of me than this, Brent. I'm attracted to you, that's all." Her decision to banish Brent from her life wavered.

A long pause followed. Brent searched her face. "Okay. I have one last chance." He hung his head.

"What?"

"The third date." He grinned mischievously. "I have one

last chance to overpower you with wonder, then take you on other dates."

"Brent, I don't know about the dates." She needed to get away from this man who erased any sane thought from her head.

"Tomorrow. Alisha wants to take Jason and Gabe to Acadia National Park. Did she ask?"

"Yes, Gabe wants to go."

"Good. I claim the day as mine for the third date. Alisha picks up Gabe at noon. I'll be here right after. Dress casually jeans and T-shirts for the next date."

"A day for a date. What is the third date?"

"My surprise. Noon tomorrow." Brent rinsed out his glass, winked at her and left.

Marlo stayed on the deck watching the stars. As long as she kept it in perspective, there would be nothing wrong with the attraction she felt for Brent. It was a physical attraction, but nothing to hold her here. She couldn't let it become more than a physical attraction. She would stay here just for Gabe's sake, she convinced herself.

Chapter Six

Alisha picked up Gabe on time, and Brent's jeep pulled in right behind. He winked at her as Marlo climbed in, but gave no clue to their destination. Brent said nothing the whole way there. His irrepressible grin made Marlo restless with anticipation. He parked his Jeep on the road between the cottage and his house. Holding her hand in his, his thumb tapped out tattoos on the back of her hand. Pushing branches out of her way, they ambled down a path. Holding both hands, he helped her scramble over the rocky places. A dozen questions formed on the edge of her tongue, but she followed his quiet lead.

The path led through the trees to a clearing deep in the woods. An unfolded stadium blanket with a wine bottle, two glasses and a spread of crackers and fruit atop a picnic basket lay in the middle of the clearing. In the middle of the blanket rested a red rose. She stopped suddenly. Never had anyone done this for her.

"Is this okay?"

Her fingers pressed to her lips. It was so perfect. He thought of all this for her. "Brent, this is so romantic. The blanket, the wine, trees, beautiful day. It's so perfect."

His grin returned. "The trees and the beautiful day, I worked the hardest on." Again, he calmly took her hand, led her to blanket. Even the feel of his palm nestled in hers was exciting. His hand was not a demand or a direction, but a consideration of movement.

She studied Brent's physique beside her. He was guileless. She was safe with Brent in a way she never had been. Trust was the key emotion. She could learn to adopt that emotion for herself if she stayed near him.

She sat cross-legged across from him on the blanket. He still held her hand and rubbed his thumb back and forth on her palm.

"You okay?"

She mutely nodded.

"I didn't ask, will you drink wine at a picnic?"

She nodded.

"Do you talk?"

A smile. Her face lost its shocked look. The smile he loved to see lit up her face. "This is nice, Brent. It took some time, some thought."

He handed her the glass, then cut a piece of cheese and handed it to her. "Wanted something special. I thought we need to get to know each other."

"Brent, the things about me, you don't know. You …" She pulled her knees up and wrapped her arms around them.

"I know. Things you've buried worry you. That's obvious." He brushed crackers from the corner of her lip. "I want to be with you. I can't wait until the barriers break to develop this relationship. Maybe if you know me better—" He brushed his thumb down her cheek. "We can progress."

He didn't add where he wanted the progression to go. She wanted to touch the hair that crept out of his collar. He stretched full length on the blanket. What would it be like to be in those arms, lie next to that muscular form? As if he could read those thoughts, he pulled her to him and wrapped her tightly within his protective arms. Her body molded against the contours of his lean body.

He stroked her cheek with a finger then traced her jaw line.

Following an instinctive need of her own, she pushed his T-shirt up, and stroked the bare chest she had wanted to touch for days. She watched his eyes as she placed her hand on his belly, then ran her fingers across the taut stomach. His pupils dilated, his breathing intensified. She'd never been this bold with Tony, never undressed him or touched where she wanted.

Brent stretched forward and in one quick movement, tugged his shirt over his head and tossed it on the ground beside him.

Marlo withheld a gasp at his nakedness, which initiated a surge of desire. She stroked the curls on his chest. Touching him was exotic. Slowly, her hands skimmed either side of his body.

The short intake of his breath as she slid fingers across his chest and down his belly moved her to further exploration. The languid movement of exploring his body, the hardness of his toned muscles, and the softness of his body hairs aroused her sending jolts of pleasure. She immersed herself in the tactile knowledge of his body. Leaning down she rubbed her cheek along the hairline. Pine needles and the smell of salt air were smells she would forever associate with Brent. A half smile, his closed eyes indicated he enjoyed the touching.

"Is this okay? Should I ..."

He leaned on his side, his eyes roved over her body. He turned her on her back and deftly flipped her shirt over her head.

"See how long you hold still for a massage."

Instinctively, she covered her body and folded her arms. He began with her arms. Like a masseuse, he rubbed her arms between his hands creating a friction then with his fingers he massaged her temples, her throat, her shoulders. Her arms fell to her side.

She felt her shoulders relax and the tension ooze out through her toes. She closed her eyes and enjoyed the calming effect of his fingers. He slowly unbuttoned the front of her shirt. He unclipped the front of her bra and quite easily cast aside her clothing until it lay in a pile on top of his. He slipped his arm beneath her and drew her to him, her nakedness pressing into his chest. Marlo kissed his shoulder blade. He skimmed his fingers lightly against her back. He kissed the side of her cheek, followed that kiss with several down her throat to her breast. Her body ached with need as his fingers, lips and tongue played her body into frenzy of desire.

The palm of his hand flowed smoothly over her belly. His thumbs flipped over her nipples sending raw ripples throughout her body. He paused, circled her nipple with this thumb, then rolled it between his thumb and finger.

His tongue followed the onslaught. She gasped. Encouraged by the sound, he sucked the other nipple. Her dormant sexuality was awakened as his hands deftly explored her body. His palms stroked the inside of arms, down her side to her thighs. His touch, the flatness and strength in his palm unnerved her. Her body, through a life of its own, moved with his sensuous rhythms. He unsnapped her jeans and tugged them down. Just as his hands had massaged her arms, they tortured her thighs with slow circling movement that made Marlo rock her hips. Her breath came in short pants.

When his thumb found the wetness between her legs and flicked across her mound, she cried out. The delightful torture was too much. Her body arched to his touch as one finger plunged inside her. She moved against the fingers in an endless rhythm.

"Easy, lady. We have time. Time to enjoy."

Enjoy. The swirls of pleasure circled around her body. How could one man find those spots in her body that rocked her? She melted in shuddering ecstasy. Wave after wave of pleasure spiraled down her entire body. Moans accompanied these sensations as his fingers created pure magic. Fireworks erupted inside as his fingers and tongue ignited pleasure points. She exploded in cries and raw passion, and bright bursts of pleasure shook her body.

He held her tight against his chest as she struggled to control the vibrations rocking her body. "Long time for you?"

"Never like that." Slowly, her breath came in short gasps. How unselfishly he had plied her body and taken her to incredible heights. She gulped in spasmodic gasps as she attempted to quiet the waves undulating throughout her body.

She had never been that bold, that desirous, that needy. "We can't do that again, Brent." She gazed past him to a spot in the woods.

"You didn't like it. I could tell."

He didn't get it; he joked. "No, no, I ..." She didn't know what to do. She had loved every torrid moment. If she followed these thoughts, she would roll over on top of him and start again. His gentle stroking of her chest excited her again. "Brent, I ..."

His tongue sought hers as he buried her protests in a kiss.

For a moment, lost in the sensations, she leaned into him and sought the closeness of his chest. Her hand stroked his shoulders, chest and back. She couldn't get enough of him.

"Marlo. I want you. Want to be with you." He whispered in her ear as he leaned his head on top of hers. "We need to know each other. Okay? This was a special day."

She nodded silently into his chest. Brent was different. She didn't want this to end. She wanted Brent wanted more of these moments. She wanted to let herself know him more. He still held her close. She remained motionless as if time had stopped. His hand gently ran across her shoulders and down her spine. He rubbed his chin across the top of her head. Her breath still came in soft gasps. Brent didn't say anything, but gently held her close, softly touching and letting her set the pace.

She leaned back on the blanket, and gazed up at him.

"You're an incredible woman, Marlo Saunders. So much unexpected from you. So many layers to the person who is Marlo." He slid his finger along her jaw line to her chin and then traced feathery patterns on her lips. She closed her eyes to savor the sensations of his touch. The warmth of the July sun shone through the trees and added to the internal fires.

When she opened her eyes, Brent held out a glass of wine. "A picnic, remember? I promised a picnic. You eat and drink at a picnic."

She sat up. She fumbled for her clothes. Brent unrolled her discarded shirt and helped her trembling fingers rebutton the front. He stretched his T-shirt over his head and sat down beside her. He handed her the plate with crackers, cheese and fruit.

"You promised a day of wonder and you succeeded." She reached for his hand. She held the back of his hand next to her cheek and closed her eyes savoring the moment. What a day.

"Any amount of wonder to please the lady. Remember the next date depends on making this a remarkable day."

He traced her lips with his fingers. "After this, do you want more."

"Oh yes, more." The smile on her lips promised much more.

"Me, too." He handed her another cracker. He sat cross-legged next to her and raised his glass. "To more enchanting dates."

She touched her glass against his. "Yes." She was glad she hadn't followed her impulse to leave. Never had anyone elicited such a passionate reaction. Maybe staying here would be better for her.

The picnic progressed in quiet conversation and gentle stroking. Marlo didn't think she would ever tire of running her hands across Brent's rugged frame. A sudden chilly breeze alerted Marlo to the amazing passage of time. The woods' dusky shades and deepening colors surprised her. Time had stopped for her. Yet, the colors indicated the afternoon had passed unnoticed.

"Brent." She pushed him back. "I need to go home. The town will talk. We can't spend the entire day here."

He studied her face. "This is a beginning, Marlo. I want you in my arms. I want you."

She mutely nodded.

"You okay?"

She smiled and fingered the soft hairs on his chest. "Yes, Brent. Fine." A fine life began in Maine and had been electrified in the Maine woods. Caught in the glory of the moment, Marlo's fears and doubts were driven away.

They talked about the cottage on the way back. He walked her to the door. Again, they paused. He touched her cheek, then kissed her. He handed her the red rose bud.

"Thank you for the day. You're a special lady. Sweet dreams. Call you in the morning."

She leaned against the door frame, her heart still pounding. The smile remained. She walked to her spot near the bay and sat on her rock.

The day had taken an amazing turn. She hadn't called Miriam, but after her magical day, she wasn't sure she would. Her body still tingled from the sweet torture of Brent's fingers. Could she create moans and needs in Brent the way he had her?

She chuckled to herself. The next date would be hers, and she certainly would try. The sun dipped low on the horizon.

Gabe would be home soon. Lazily, she walked to the kitchen door. Would Gabe settle for boxed macaroni and cheese? She flipped on the kitchen light and screamed.

Chapter Seven

"Hello, my charming wife." Tony grabbed her arm and yanked her to his chest. "Seeing someone else?" He held her chin in his hand. His black eyes glinted. The smell of his aftershave, the touch of his fingers nauseated her. "I see you missed me." He slapped her snapping her head back. She bit her lip, but didn't cry.

"How did you find me? You're in prison," she said. She winced waiting for the other blow.

"I got out. Surprised to see me after what you did? I've missed my love. Think I couldn't follow your trail? Been watching you for days." He tore the rose from her grasp, digging the thorns across her palm.

"No!" She reached for the rose.

"A memento of your time with him?" He tossed it on the floor and ground it with his heel. "He's history. Get Gabe's things. His clothes, his baseball card books. I'm taking him."

"No! We have a life here. Leave him. Leave us. You and I are divorced. We're not part of your life now."

He twisted her arm behind her until she bent to the floor. "I know you missed me. You want to be with Gabe? "

"Please, Tony." She could barely get the words out. "What do you want?"

He tightened his grip until he heard another gasp. "Lover boy sure made you forgot me fast. Your lips are swollen, your hair disheveled. Must have been some date. Does he know he's fooling with a married woman?"

She wrenched her arm free, moved away and faced him. "I'm not yours. We're divorced. I am not that woman anymore."

"Yes, beauty, you're mine. And I intend to enjoy what's

mine. No more is this man going to share what's mine. Not my wife, not my son. Where did you go today?"

"You've been watching us. You've been spying on that boat!" Her hand massaged her shoulder. "You are weak. All you could do is spy."

"I've been haunting you? Making you look over your shoulder? I didn't need to spy. I have contacts. I found you easy enough. So eager was I to see you and Gabe, I went from prison to here. By the time the authorities figure out what happened, Gabe and I will be long gone. You'll do what I tell you. Where's Gabe?"

"Not here."

"Where's my son?"

"Not here. He's safe. Away from you."

He grabbed the front of her blouse and yanked her to his chest. "Get him."

"Leave him alone! He's safe. He doesn't want …"

Another slap ended her words. "Doesn't want his father?"

"You're not taking Gabe. You're not taking me. You don't own me." With flattened palms, she pushed away from Tony. Her breath came in short intakes. *You have a life. Don't let him scare you.* She lifted her head and looked him directly in the eyes. "You're not taking Gabe. You're not taking me."

"Brave, aren't we?" He moved in never losing the eye contact.

Marlo clenched her teeth to keep from shaking. *He has no hold over you.* "I don't need you anymore, Tony DeFalco." Her words came out in a strained whisper. She flinched as his hand swiftly reached her, but he unbuttoned the top button of her shirt and paused.

"Who's taking care of you now? You can't do anything without help." His fingers slid down the front of her cleavage.

"I can. I can drive. I don't need you." She stepped back away from his touch. A vision of the patience Miriam had exhibited as she taught Marlo to drive added to her determination. Miriam encouraged her newfound courage and to risk a fresh start. "I don't need you." She repeated to reinforce her bravado.

"Who's the man taking care of you now? The one who just left."

"He's the police chief." She hardened her expression. "Even you can't entangle with the police … not as a fugitive. You aren't the man he is."

Tony grabbed a handful of her hair and brought her to her knees in front of him. "Don't need me. Banging the police chief, you little slut. You're mine. Get my son and what's mine."

Marlo twisted to relieve to wrenching of her head. The sound of tires on gravel brought them both to a standstill.

Brent! She closed her eyes. *Please, stay away.*

Tony dragged her to her feet and pulled her in front of him. "How cute. You're still alone and he comes to see you. Wants more of his little slut does he?" He faced the door. Marlo felt the jab in her ribs. *Oh my god, a gun.* "A little welcoming party for our local hero."

"Brent, go!" Her warning only encouraged Brent to shove open the door with his shoulder.

"Welcome, Chief!" Tony waved his gun. "Toss down your gun and she doesn't bloody up the kitchen."

Brent looked to Marlo then Tony. He flung her denim jacket to the floor and held up his arms, his palms facing outward. "I only have her jacket."

Tony sneered. "What kind of chief goes without his weapon?"

Although he spoke to Tony, he studied Marlo's face. She couldn't give him answers now. "Trenton, Maine, isn't the kind of town you need to be constantly armed in."

Marlo felt the tension in Tony dissolve. His grasp on her arm loosened. "Let him go, Tony. He knows nothing. He's nothing to you."

"Ahh." Tony laughed and jerked her around. "But he is to you. Let's see what you're willing to do to protect him."

Marlo froze. A kind, innocent man was in danger because of her thoughtlessness. Once again, she had chosen a course of disaster. Now she, Gabe and Brent were in trouble. Or at least, Gabe was safe.

"Who are you and what do you want? She has very little here you would want. Leave now." Brent's stance, legs apart was a courageous, authoritative pose.

"No, sir." Tony sneered. "You know little about her. She

is a woman with a shady past. Shouldn't have been involved with another man, a cop no less." He yanked Marlo back by the hair until she faced his grimacing face. "Thought a cop would protect you, is that why you flaunted yourself in front of him? I saw those skinny, cutoffs showing him your legs, those tight tops. Thought you might interest him?" He yanked harder until she cried out.

Brent advanced until Tony waved the gun. "Back." He snarled. "You can't protect her. Don't try anything foolish. You'll die for a woman who isn't worth it."

Tears formed in her eyes. Tony again would control her life. Her new start had failed. She had to save Gabe from his father and get Brent out of this. Abruptly, Tony let go of her hair, but wrenched her arm behind her back.

"Over here," he ordered. He moved away from the door until they stood between the kitchen and Great Room. "I can watch both doors in case Mr. Chief here has friends." Brent stood warily atop the step separating the two rooms. Marlo couldn't make eye contact with him.

"Tony, you can't do this. He can't help you. Let him go."

"Ahh, how precious you are thinking you have a say. Thinking you can save him. How brave you are. More spunk, Marlo?" He tugged on her arm. "You won't defy me, will you, Marlo? We'll wait until Gabe gets here."

"What do you want? What do you intend to do with us?" Brent leaned nonchalantly against the counter and rested his foot on the chair. From Marlo's angle, she saw the ankle holster. Did he always carry a gun? Had he had that on dates? She met his eyes. A steely blue steady gaze concentrated on Tony. Brent was a man to be reckoned with, edgy, aware. A side she hadn't seen. If he tried for that gun, Tony would kill him. Tony had no morals, no fears. Brent wouldn't have a chance. Neither would Gabe if he returned. She had to act. No more passive Marlo letting things happen to her.

"You'll never get Gabe. I won't let you." She ground out.

"And just will you do to stop me, little Marlo? Fight me?" He spun her to face him. "You'll do exactly as I tell you just as you've always done." He stood between her and Brent. With that perspective, he could easily mow either one of them down. "We'll wait for Gabe. Then we'll stage a little lovers' quarrel between the two of you. Kill you both and make it look like the good police chief here found out what a worthless piece Marlo really is." He faced Marlo again. "You've lost your appeal, Marlo. You're used material now. Used by our chief here, weren't you? Came home, flushed with carnal pleasures. I don't need you."

She saw Brent lean down. For the gun? In a instant, Tony turned. She screamed, "No!" She leaped for Tony's arm. Two shots rang out. She felt a burning pain in her side, then blackness.

•

She awakened in hospital whiteness.

"Miss Saunders, can you hear me?"

She moaned and instinctively grabbed her side.

"Miss Saunders, you can't do that. You've only been out of surgery an hour."

Another face appeared. The faces blurred, then cleared.

"Water," she whispered. A hand stretched a straw to her. "Gabe?"

"He's fine. He's with Alisha."

"I know you are hurting, Miss Saunders, but can you answer questions."

She struggled to focus on the faces. A blue uniform leaned forward. She could not place the face.

"I'm Patti Closeman." The blue uniform moved closer, her hand rested on the bed. "Can you remember anything? It's important to the case."

Images of Brent, Gabe, Tony and the cottage swirled together. She flinched as the echo of a gunshot resounded in her head.

"I've never seen a dead body either. It must be frightening."

Marlo's eyes widened. "Dead? Brent!"

"The intruder was killed."

Tears streamed unheeded down her cheeks. Tony. Dead. Never to hurt her or Gabe again.

Patti patted her arm. "I know this is upsetting, but we need some answers for Brent's case. Could you at least nod or shake your head if I ask you questions?"

Marlo nodded.

"Brent said when he returned, an intruder had a gun to your head."

Marlo nodded. Details blurred together.

"The intruder threatened you and Brent O'Neill."

She remembered. The gun cocked then she couldn't remember.

"In Brent's report—" Patti looked at the file on her lap. "You pushed the intruder. He missed Brent, but turned and shot you. Brent shot him, which is why the intruder missed you with the second shot."

Marlo nodded again. She remembered jumping for Tony. All that anger. She would have killed him if she could.

Tears continued silently down her cheeks and she did nothing to stop them. Brent saved her life. Tony was dead. What had Gabe seen when he returned? His father. Gabe would have given away the secret. The policewoman had only referred to Tony as an intruder; Tony had not been identified. What had she said about investigating Brent? Questions pounded in her head but she was too weak to work them out. Maybe later …

•

Brent watched her sleep. She hadn't awakened when he conned the nurse into letting him come in. He sat beside her and stoked her arm. She was alive. Parts of the puzzle that made up the woman Marlo Saunders were more evident, but he was still unsure how to piece them together. When would she trust him enough to tell him what happened with that intruder before he got there? What troubled her sleep now?

"Gabe?" was her first word.

"Safe with Alisha and my family. It's okay." He stroked her hair away from her face. Vivid bruises marred her cheek. What would that man have done to her if he hadn't had a sense of trouble and had returned to the cottage?

"Did Gabe see anything?"

"No, he wasn't there. We haven't let him back in the cottage. There are bullet holes in the wall."

Marlo shuddered.

"You are coming home with me when they release you. You

are one brave lady."

The kindness of Brent's stroking calmed her. She tried to block images, but the picture of Tony as he aimed his gun returned.

"The FBI is after that intruder. Tony Defalco has a long list with crimes division. We can't figure out what he was doing in Maine. Not his line. The FBI is in on the investigation of my case."

"Your case? FBI?"

"I killed a man, Marlo. I was off duty. FBI wanted this guy. They will help with the case."

"Here? Who?" She struggled to sit up.

"Don't panic. You did nothing wrong. Lie down." He pressed her shoulder.

"Are you in any trouble? You saved me from … trouble."

Brent frowned. "I'm sure it will get straightened out. Rest. We'll discuss this when we get home."

After Brent left, she couldn't rest. The FBI? Her refuge in Maine was gone. Tony had obliterated her life again. What would Brent think of her when he found out what her life had been, when he discovered that he had killed her ex-husband? She couldn't face Brent ever again. She had she no way of getting out of this hospital and the area. The door opened. A familiar female figure appeared. Now she could get out.

"You're fine, Marlo, Tony's dead. We'll get you out of the heat." Miriam's firm voice ordered the changes she needed. Her world faded.

Soon Marlo was whisked away and protected by Miriam Allen who had helped her after Tony's arrest. For a week, Marlo went through the mechanics of sleeping, showering, picking at the delivered food. Each time she and Miriam went over the details of Tony's death, Marlo's world sank lower.

There's no going back. The woman who faced her in the mirror had the hang dog look of defeat. Bruises still showed around her temple and forehead. Her eye, now open, still had memories of swelling and bruises. Tony was dead, but so was her thin, shaky tether on freedom. What now?

Miriam appeared behind her. "You can stay here until you recover, but you can't hide in this motel forever. It's been two weeks, Marlo. Lunch is delivered."

Marlo followed Miriam to the open family room. Two unmade beds reminded her of the living conditions. Gabe listlessly sprawled across one of the beds watching television. No more fishing trips. Marlo's sigh came from her toes down through her body. She poured herself a cup of coffee then followed Miriam to the secluded deck off the back of the room.

"Look at what you're doing to Gabe. He says little. He's listless. You could go back."

Marlo shook her head. She couldn't face Brent. The lies she represented. Tiny Trenton with its safe streets wouldn't welcome a stranger with a past.

"You misjudged your policeman. He visited you every day in the hospital." Miriam held back her wearied sigh. She had this conversation before. Marlo refused to have anything to do with her friends in Trenton, especially her Brent O'Neill.

Marlo shook her head again. "Something is still not right. It's not over." She swallowed back the fear that haunted her still. "I caused grave danger, almost death." The words choked her as she uttered them. "Almost death for friends, for Gabe."

"Marlo, Tony's dead. Go on with your life. That past is gone." Miriam touched her arm.

"It's not over. I feel … danger. No one will be safe. I feel …danger. The shadow on my life is still there. Find me another place. One far from neighbors, friends, anyone who could be hurt by me. I don't want to see Brent." She slouched back to the isolation of the bathroom.

Later that week, as Miriam sat at her desk, Marlo's words still ringing in Miriam's ears. Nothing could dissuade Marlo. Her fears kept her from reaching out. She looked at the map sites she had chosen. Marlo still needed to be watchful. Tony had made friends in prison, but nothing indicated they talked about Marlo or that anyone would be interested in her. Tony was dead. Total isolation was not what she or her son needed. Her door slammed against her wall interrupting her thoughts.

Marlo's police chief glowered at her over the top of her desk. "What's going on here?" he demanded. "Where is Marlo? Gabe? My sister said you picked him up. Who the hell do you think you are?"

"Would you and your attitude sit down." Her tone was direct, she remained calm and distant, which aggravated him more. He threw the seat back and sat.

"You have no right to detain her …"

"I do." She stood. Hers was now the position of power and she was used to that power. "I am Miriam Allen and I work for the federal government." After she let that sink in, she added. "And Marlo gave me those rights." She crossed to stand near a couch in back of him. "She is safe and in a spot she doesn't want you to know. Gabe is safe and with his mother. I will protect Marlo at all costs."

Brent stared at the desktop and let the information sink in his head. "She specifically said she didn't want to see me. But you do know who I am, so she did talk about me."

"Yes, Brent, I know a great deal about you." The woman walked back to the desk and sat across from him. "She has her reasons, Brent," she added softly. "This has been difficult for her."

He looked up. "I need to see her for myself. I'm the one who shot him."

"I know that. She will return to testify for you."

"I don't need that." He stood and leaned over her on the desk. "I want to see her. Where is she?"

"I need a statement from you about the shooting for our investigation. I won't tell you where she is. She won't see you."

He slumped in the chair. "Let's get this over with. The police have my statements."

"Had you seen Tony DeFalco before that day?"

"No, read the reports. Didn't connect the two until you guys came down and briefed us."

"Do you know anything about him … his past?'

"Was in prison. Numbers man … drug ring. Escaped. Bought his way out. Fled to Maine. Fled here to … " He stopped. Flashes of the day in the cottage. Tony, Marlo. His words to her. He gave Miriam a sidelong glance, then continued. Each word came out slowly. "He came here deliberately."

She nodded. "He was after Marlo and Gabe."

"Why?" This was too incredible. He paced. "How?"

"Tony was her husband. Gabe's father."

He stopped, gripped the back of the chair. "I shot her husband?" He sat back down. The man wasn't a robber. He hurt Marlo. "Her husband?"

"*Was.* Six months ago, the divorce was official. She testified against him, then fled for her own protection."

"Under witness protection?"

She stood and moved around the desk. "No, she didn't qualify. She's committed no crimes. She didn't know much about Tony's operations."

"I was so stupid." He bent his head down and studied the dirty tile on the floor. "For a cop. I missed critical elements. The familiarity between them in the house. She knew his moves. She tried to protect me and it almost cost her life." He felt Miriam's eyes upon him. He met her gaze. "I made mistakes here."

She nodded. "If your feelings are involved, it's tough to be objective."

Brent shook his head. Again in his life he'd missed clues. He should have paid more attention to Marlo's doubts. It all made sense now. She was waiting, fearing Tony would show up.

"Did she have any idea of Tony's illegal activities?"

"Not when she married him. She was too young, too naive. Later, she suspected, but wasn't quite sure what he was involved in. She realized things weren't right."

"Why didn't she leave? How did she get involved with him?" He looked up. "The bruises. He must have been a brute."

"You'll have to ask her about her early life."

"You're protective." He stood near the windows looked down on Portland's streets. "I can't ask her. She won't let me, remember?"

"We became friends when we worked together when Tony was arrested." She stood beside him. "She tried to escape once. He caught her. She ended up with a broken jaw. Gabe was always Tony's deterrent. I think why he wanted a child was so he could control her. There were other horrors. She's ..."

"A very brave woman. She was shot protecting me, I'm sure

now."

"Brent." She placed his hand on his arm. "Life's not been easy. She needs a rescuer."

He nodded and stared out the window. "But she won't see me."

"She's afraid you will think less of her or pity her."

"What?" He swung around to face her.

"You've reached her. You're important in her life. And you may be her only way out … She can't go back."

"Is she in danger?"

"Physically? No, we don't think so. We … Tony's friends looked for Tony when he escaped. They didn't seem to think that Marlo was important."

"'Think,' 'seem' are vague terms. You don't know, do you?"

"She knew little of his business. She wasn't involved. I don't think anyone will disturb her. Her danger is her own mental anguish. She's made attachments in Maine. Gabe's happiness, which influences her the most."

"And me? What did she say about me?"

Miriam walked back to the desk. "You are part of her conversations. Gabe talks about you always. What she chooses to do from here …"

"Why can't you tell me where she is? I need to help her. To see her. You seem to be close to her. You know what she thinks."

"We're staying together. She cares for you."

"Can I follow you home? I need to see she is okay." Brent stood before her. He wanted to shake her to make her understand. Her eyes showed compassion for him.

"She told me … begged me not to tell you."

"Why?" He tugged on his hair in the front. "I don't understand. She finally trusts me. She … We … I need to see her."

"She needs you. I know that. I don't know if she knows that. I came here to help her, not as part of the investigating team."

He grabbed Miriam hand and held it between his palms. He searched her eyes for a clue. "We both care about her … love her. Help me."

"You love her?"

"Yes." He let go of the hand and commenced his endless pacing. "Thoughts of her with his gun on her. Our relationship. If I could —"

"Does she know?"

"No." He shook his head and ruffled his dark hair with his fingers. "I figured it out recently. Never had a chance to tell her."

Miriam reached in her desk, rummaged through the drawer and pulled out a pack of matches with "The Courtyard" printed in bold letters and an address printed on the flap. She flipped them deftly to Brent's hand. "Here. Room 208, back corner. Isolated cabins."

He nodded. "Thanks. You didn't tell me. I'm a detective by profession. I notice things." He tucked the matches in his pocket before he left.

Chapter Eight

The car door slamming startled her as did every loud noise, every sudden move. Gabe slept peacefully on the couch. Wincing, Marlo slowly walked to the door. Her side still hurt. The scar of the bullet would be another lifelong reminder of Tony. She padded shakily toward the door.

She hadn't slept in days. Her clothes were disheveled and ill-fitting. The only clothes she had were ones she and Miriam had acquired from used clothing shops. Her own clothes were still at the cottage. She couldn't get herself to go back. The cottage and its memories were too much. Memories of Brent. His kisses. His kindness. Her new life. Tony destroyed that life when he appeared. She couldn't return a convict's wife, a dealer's wife. Brent had almost lost his life because of her.

Miriam did not appear at the door as she did every day. She was the only one to come back to this spot. She peered out the curtains. A green Jeep parked outside was not Miriam's. Brent stood staring at the door. She walked out.

"She told you?"

"No, I'm a thorough cop. I follow my leads."

His stance portrayed anger. His feet spaced wide apart, his hands on hips. His lips formed a thin line. No ready smile. No blue eyes dancing. Was he angry about her lying? Or for not being the woman she pretended to be? She owed him an explanation.

"I'll be there for your hearing Thursday. I'm not leaving until it's over. I wouldn't let you down." The last line caught in her throat. The image of Tony's gun going off flashed in her mind. She and Gabe owed him their lives.

"Only the hearing? Come back to Trenton with me, Marlo."

He moved forward, but didn't reach out to touch her. "Come home."

"Brent, I can't." Her heart ached. She wanted to fling herself into his reassuring arms but she couldn't stay in Trenton now. "I'm sorry."

He crossed the distance in one stride and held her close to his chest.

"Brent, I can't expose you to dangers. I'm not the woman…" His kiss broke up her sentence and her thoughts.

"I need you more than just in that hearing." He stopped as she caught her breath. "If I ever lost you …"

She attempted to move away, but he held her fast in his arms.

"What will people in Trenton think now that Tony's history is out?"

"People didn't know you when you were with Tony. The only Marlo they know is Gabe's beautiful loving mom who moved to Trenton and makes great desserts." His blue eyes were compelling. "Come back to Trenton with me.

She left his tight grip. "I was married to a criminal. My life before, my connection with Tony…" She wiped the tears back with her sleeve.

He put his arm around her shoulder. "Must have been hard for all those years. Tony's gone. Your ghosts are gone. Come Back to Trenton. I can help you get past all of this. Trust me."

"I can't trust myself." She paced the small gravel drive between them. "Can't let go of feeling of the constant alertness, constantly looking over my shoulder. It kept me alive those years with Tony. It's not a feeling you can shake."

"I can protect you." He held her hands preventing her movement away from him. She stared at the gravel.

"I can't let you just protect me." She looked into his eyes. How could she explain? Brent with his caring family, his own sense of confidence had nothing to compare to the worlds she had known. How would he understand? "My life has been filled with those who 'helped' me. My aunt who told me what to do, Tony who demanded obedience. I can't." She struggled to explain. "When I rebelled and decided for myself, I made bad decisions. I'm afraid to trust any decision I make. I need time to learn."

"Leaving Tony wasn't a bad decision. Moving here wasn't a bad thing."

"Leaving Tony almost killed you."

He stroked her cheek. His kindness was almost her undoing. "Was I a mistake? Was our developing relationship a mistake in your life?"

"No," she whispered. "Oh Brent, I don't know. What do I have to offer you? What if Tony's deeds follow me? What is this feeling I can't shake? What if I endanger you again? I don't know what to risk, what decision is the right one. I can't afford bad decisions again. Too many people get hurt."

He carefully held her hands between his. "You'll never know by running. Gabe loves it in Trenton." He knew the unfairness of using Gabe as a leveraging tool. "Your past isn't important to me. You are. Come home. The past Marlo DeFalco isn't the who bewitched me."

"I wasn't that Marlo once. I was weak, passive. I should have stood up to him. I should have."

He held her face in his palms. "Marlo." He looked directly in her eyes. "You are a brave woman. I am honored to be with you. Your past, that Marlo, did what she needed to survive. Be the Marlo Saunders of Maine. I can't let go of you in my life." He pleaded watching her eyes. He had to convince her.

Words wouldn't come out. A battle ranged between her feelings for Brent and her ungrounded fears and connection to her past.

"Marlo, give us a chance."

She couldn't leave him. She had nowhere she wanted to go except Trenton. She nodded. "Gabe's asleep inside."

"Let's go wake him. Take him home. We can find another spot."

She shook her head. "Gabe wants the cottage. Good memories." She blushed. Good memories for her, too. A vision of Brent and a picnic blanket had haunted her for days. She had her own memories attached to the cottage. "Gabe needs to go back there. I can …"

"Come back. I've cleaned up the cottage. No signs of an altercation."

"I need to wait for Miriam. Say goodbye."

He quietly touched her arm. "Promise me you won't disappear again. You will come home. I will be waiting in the cottage. I will have dinner ready."

She smiled and touched his cheek. "Thank you, Brent, for being you. Understanding. Caring."

"Dinner at six." He kissed her, then kissed her on her forehead. "I do love you, Marlo. Believe that. The rest is easy."

When she arrived, Brent waited in the middle of the driveway. The cottage looked the same as the day she first arrived with Brent. Nestled among the trees with the ocean behind, it looked picture perfect. Alisha and Jason came in close behind them. Jason and Gabe ran off to the water. The return was not traumatic to Gabe. Marlo hesitated at the door. Walking slowly into the kitchen had a dizzying effect. Contrasting pictures of the picnic, Brent on a blanket, Tony, the gun firing all swam before her. Patches on the wall separating the room from the bedroom hallway were the only reminders of the fight.

"You okay?" Alisha followed at her elbow as she walked from one room to another.

She nodded.

"You can stay with one of us."

"No, I've stopped running from my past. Any ghosts I need to face are here. I have to deal with it."

"Good," Alisha relaxed and offered. "Registration for school is tomorrow. We can go tomorrow."

"I can do that now." Gabe could start school. She could register him without fear. They had a place. Out the window she could see Gabe, Brent and Jason skipping stones across the water.

"Brent ask you about the wedding?" Alisha plopped in the dining room chair so she also could look out at the water.

"What?" Her heart stopped at the mention of the word "wedding."

"My sister marries in two weeks in Bennington, Vermont. She wants you to come to the wedding. You have an invitation here in your mail."

"A wedding invitation. She doesn't know me."

"You're family now. We have told her all about you." Alisha played with the mat on the table.

She didn't pursue what they had said. "I don't fit in the family. My name isn't in order." She smiled. She liked this family.

"Oh yeah, tell that to Jake, Karl, or Lee and Neal, my in-laws."

The line sunk in. She moaned. "There's no I or M or F or G."

Alisha avoided eye contact. "Ericka is marrying Ian. You are Marlo."

She moaned again. "Was I invited simply because of my beginning letter of my name? Is that why you're so nice to me?"

Alisha laughed. "No, Brent likes you. Jason likes Gabe and you. I have more fun with you than with my sisters. Maybe it was fate. You fit here because of the letter. Believe in the fate. Come to the wedding. You and I are going shopping. I need something new. You can help. You need to work on now. Let go of yesterday. This is a start."

A wedding with the O'Neill crew was enticing. "Does Brent know about this?

"I don't know if we asked him, but he will want you there. He was so worried about you and Gabe when he couldn't see you. Thought about nothing else. When he remembers about the wedding, he'll ask. Won't go without you. It will be a long time until he lets you out of his sight."

She looked at Alisha. It would be fun. Shopping. The wedding. "Okay."

The adjustment back to the town was as easy as adjusting to being with O'Neill crew. Brent's family made a steady stream of stops at her door to check if she needed anything. Mrs. Carlson, her neighbor, brought snacks for Gabe. The town turned out a welcome mat and talked with her, asked about her.

She breathed relief and most of her fears died. Although a persistent doubt still plagued her, she pushed aside her foreboding cloud each time it surfaced. Her plans overshadowed her doubts for a while.

Gabe and Jason anticipated the opening of school. She and

Alisha registered the boys, then shopped for school supplies.

Reading, watching the weather channel, baking and reading to Gabe filled her evenings and created a calm ending to her days. A late night thunderstorm interrupted her peace. Lightning slashed across the bay lighting up trees and branches. Figures appeared in the spiny forms of branches lit up by the storm. Thunder drowned any other sounds. She held her breath and listened to the ticking of the grandfather's clock to compose herself. The room that had been her haven became ominous. The patches left over from the bullet holes leered at her. She wiped her palms on her jeans and paced the length of the great room.

He's dead. No one is here, but Gabe and me. No ghosts. The lights flashed off. She froze in her spot. Gabe! She fumbled for matches in the kitchen desk and used a candle to light her way from the kitchen to the bedroom. Gabe slept fitfully, unaware of the menacing shadows and frightening crashes of thunder.

Another loud clap of thunder was enough. She found her flashlight and her keys. Wrapping Gabe tightly in his quilt, she wove her way to the car. Lightning lit up the roadways as the rain cascaded down on the car roof. Her hair plastered on her face, her shirt clinging to her, she knocked at Brent's door.

"Marlo." Brent grabbed Gabe, unwrapped the wet quilt and laid him on the couch. He covered him with a dry Afghan.

"The cottage—shadows on the wall, the patch, " she babbled as he toweled her hair dry.

"Shh." He kissed her cheek. "I'm here. Let's get you out of those wet clothes. You stay here." Standing her in front of a warm fire, he peeled layers of wet clothes from her and wrapped her in a terry robe and soft blanket. He rubbed her back until her shivering stopped. They sat in front of the fire.

Her teeth still chattering, she tried to explain. "The cottage, Tony's face—I couldn't stand it in this storm."

"You have been brave long enough. It's time to let down."

She snuggled close to his warmth and his strong chest. "Brent, I'm sorry."

"I'm glad you came." The earnestness in his voice reassured her.

•

She awoke in Brent's bed. The small bed still held the warmth of Brent's body. The comfort of his arms still lingered although he was no longer there. Gabe slept on the other side of her. She stretched full length. In the light of day, the lightning flashes and images of her husband's face were less vivid. She rubbed her face against the pillow still indented in the image of Brent's head. She closed her eyes and savored the warmth of the bed and lingering feel of Brent's arms. This was how life should be. She squeezed her eyelids shut. If she could just as easily squeeze away her sense of foreboding. Get rid of the evil shadow that dogged her life. She stretched again warding away her fears and evil sensors. The smell of coffee pulled from the warm cocoon of Brent's bed. She found Brent in the kitchen.

"Sleep okay?"

"Brent, I didn't mean to disturb you last night."

"You came where you know you were safe. That says a lot." He rubbed her shoulder then pulled her into the folds of his arms. "You need to deal with ghosts, but you need to know when to ask for help." He kissed the top of her head. "You trusted me enough to come here in the middle of the night. That's a big step."

She nestled her cheek next to his shirt. It would be so easy to just stay here. Let all her fears and doubts melt away just in the security of his arms.

He paused. "Move in here. Gabe would like it."

"I can't." She startled as if he had read her mind. It wasn't proper to do that. "I can't live with you in this small town. You're the police chief. We chastely shared that bed last night. It wouldn't stay that way. What could I tell Gabe?" She moved away and gripped the counter.

He poured her a cup of coffee. "Will you come here when you need to?"

She sipped the coffee. "Yes, Brent, I need you … I want to be with you."

He dumped sugars into his cup and rapidly stirred, clinking the spoon against the side. He was inches from her and she felt the warmth of his body. "I want you, Marlo. Last night, having you curled against me was torture and delight. I want you now."

She gripped her cup. Awaking in his bed had her senses tingling. She wanted to be cradled in his arms and taste and touch him. As if moved by the same thought, they moved to each other.

Taking his face in both her hands, she kissed him with the passion she felt inside. He moved closer and trapped her body next to his. His needs were apparent as his body pressed against hers.

"Mommy, how did we get here? Hi Brent!" Gabe's' voice forced them apart.

"Ahh, it rained last night," Brent answered and directed Gabe's attention to him as Marlo tightened the robe around her and picked up her cup.

"The lights went off so we came here. We slept in Brent's bed." Her hands still rested on the knot of her robe. Her body cried in need, but tomorrow was another day. She sighed. Coming here had soothed her fears, but it had awakened her desires.

Going home with Gabe would force her to focus on the immediate needs: Gabe, her new life. When she had last talked with Miriam, they had discussed finding Marlo a job. Marlo needed to search the papers and learn basic skills. Maybe if she were busy she wouldn't think of Brent or the power of his hands and the tantalizing feel of his tongue.

"Great. Can we go outside! Lots of branches and stuff all over."

"As soon as I dress, I think we need to go to our own place."

Once home, Gabe plowed down the hill to access the damage to his favorite spots. She closed her eyes and willed herself to let him go without warnings, without following to assure herself he was fine. *It's a new life.* If she made that her mantra, maybe her lingering fears would end haunting her. Marlo cautiously opened the door. No glaring shadows, no frightening images. She flung open the door. Sunshine poured in the doors of the deck. She glanced at the plaster covering the bullet holes. Reminders.

The phone rang. She smiled. Brent checking up on her. She

answered the phone, "I'm home and not afraid." She wandered to the deck doors. "Brent?" The only response was heavy breathing. "Hello? Who's there?" A loud click. She fingered the phone. Wrong number, that's all. She dialed Brent.

"Hi, Beautiful. I was just thinking of you curled next to me last night. And the power of just one kiss."

She smiled and hugged the phone between her ear and her shoulder. "Hi. I just needed to hear your voice."

"Anything wrong? Are you okay in that house?"

She hesitated, but decided not to mention her silliness over a wrong number. "No, I'm fine. See you later? I need a shower."

"Tonight, I'll call when I get off duty. And I'll definitely be thinking of you now in that shower."

She laughed to herself as she hung up. Life was turning. She just needed to think of that. A shower, huh. Wonder what a shower with Brent would be like?

As she rubbed her body with soap she imagined what it would be like with Brent's hands over her. She wanted touch his chest, be close to his body. She had never felt this way. She was eager to explore every inch of him and enjoy his explorations. She hummed. Just as she stepped on the bath mat, the phone rang. She wrapped the towel around her and stumbled to get it.

"Marlo DeFalco?"

"This is Marlo Saunders."

"Marlo DeFalco," the gruff voice insisted.

"Who are you?" Who would reach her here? She clutched the towel in front of her. "Who is this?" The last few words came out in a whisper. "What do you want?"

"Just you, Marlo, dear, just want you. I want my fingers in you hair. I want to touch you all over." A long pause. Marlo stared at the phone. Just before she dropped it, the voice continued. "Tell your little boy, hello." A click followed. She pressed *69 and received the message, "We cannot trace that call." She slammed down the receiver. She checked out the window. Gabe was in sight, tossed stones into the water. She looked back at the phone. Tony was dead.

Who else would ever call her? She shuddered. His tone reminded her of slime oozing down a wall. She shuddered in the cold. After another check to Gabe, she walked to her room. It was nobody, a crank call. But who would know to call her here? Who even knew Marlo DeFalco still existed.

She yanked a T-shirt over her head. It had to be nobody. Tony had crazy friends and maybe even creditors. She couldn't let her fears make a simple wrong number a critical point. But the shadow over her shoulder reappeared.

"Gabe, I need you to come in now." She stood on the deck until he was close. A single motorboat sped past. *Tony is gone.*

"Mom, do I have to?" Gabe stood beneath her amid the rocks and vegetation. "It's fun. Lots of sticks around. I could gather them for you. The waves are high still."

The motorboat purred past again. This time, slower.

"No." She watched the boat. She couldn't get to Gabe except by running down the flight of stairs at the end of the deck. The boat stopped offshore. "No, come in now." Noting the squeak in her voice, Gabe looked around. "No, I mean, we're meeting Alisha, remember? You're playing at Funtown with Josh. Come in." She motioned him to the steps. As he started up, the boat motored away. Marlo watched its retreat. So many boats in Maine.

"Mom, are you okay? You're acting funny." Gabe's anxious face peered into hers.

"No, I'm—" She ushered him inside and firmly closed the sliding door behind them. "I'm just trying to think of what dress to get for the wedding."

"Is that what you and Alisha are doing today? Get a real fancy one, Mom. You've never had one. Daddy—" Gabe halted.

Marlo knelt down. Since Tony's death, Gabe had said very little about his father or his death. "Gabe?"

"You need something pretty to celebrate." He touched her cheek. "We've never been to a wedding, have we, Mom? Our life is so much better now. We can have fun. I can make noise." He headed to his room. "Mom, Daddy wasn't very nice, was he?"

"No, Gabe. Daddy wasn't a good man. We have a better life now."

Gabe nodded. "I like it here." He trotted off to his room.

Marlo sighed deeply. *Yeah, it's okay. I'll adjust. Gabe certainly has faster than me.*

They met Alisha and Josh at a nearby mall. The two boys were given passes at Funtown. A babysitter kept their money and watched as they yelled to each. Alisha and Marlo were free to shop.

"You need something clingy, sensuous." Alisha pulled three dresses off the racks.

"For a wedding?" Marlo pulled a sedate suit from a rack.

"No, no, something like this." Alisha pushed Marlo's selection back and held a midnight blue shimmery dress. "You need something to attract attention, to make you stand out."

"Brides attract attention at weddings, not guests. I'm a stranger at this wedding."

"She can't wait to meet you."

"What's going on here? Why do I feel like a pigeon or sacrificial lamb?"

"We like you." Alisha sat on the stool and fastened the back of the dress. "We like what you do to big, bossy Brent and we want you around Brent. After Ericka's wedding, Brent's the only one not married."

Marlo spun around. "What? What are you guys thinking? I'm not going if you think this will lead to—" Her hands flew to her cheeks. Her face flushed.

Alisha sat on the stool and reached to flatten Marlo's cuff. "Look me in the eyes and tell me you are not interested in my brother."

"I ... " Her knees quavered as she sorted her emotions, she sank to a stool next to Alisha. "I want to be with Brent. I like him," she finally admitted. "But love? I don't know."

"You've had your love ideals smashed. Let time and nature take their course. Come with us. See how you feel caught up in a wedding and moments of love. Besides, it will be fun! All of us line dancing. You with all the O'Neill clan!"

"You know if I was of a sane mind, all of you would be scary."

"Compared to your other life, we are meek and mild."

Alisha's prodding produced the dress and an agreement to see what happened at the wedding. Her anticipation grew. Her fears were overshadowed.

Chapter Nine

A caravan of cars arrived at the destination at the same time. Marlo felt sorry for the future O'Neill brother-in-law, Ian. A passel of O'Neills could be disconcerting. Noise, laughter, and confusion followed in their wake. She stayed in the aunt's house with Alisha's family. She saw little of Brent until the wedding.

Brent, a wedding attendant, stood out in his tux. Broad shouldered with taut muscles straining against the tux created a standout image. A draw, especially for Marlo, was the fit of tux trousers across his butt. Her eyes were drawn to him throughout the beginning of the ceremony. A tingling in her belly every time he looked in his direction made it difficult to concentrate on the ceremony.

Gabe, who had never been to a wedding, was entranced. Ericka was as stunning as she was gracious. Meeting her was as easy as greeting the rest of the family. Standing at the altar happiness, charm and natural beauty flowed from Ericka.

A fantasy of she and Brent standing at an altar with a minister and the words "I do" invaded her thoughts. She shook her head to dispel the image. Marriage to Brent would never happen. Their lives were too different. His family had hinted an expectation of wedding plans, but Brent never indicated an interest in permanence. What did she want from him? She drove these questions from her mind and studied the bride as she floated back down the aisle.

Marlo chuckled as she threw sunflowers with the rest of the guests after the ceremony. She had rarely attended weddings. This was like playing with Barbie figures of her childhood. Brent appeared at her side and put a protective arm around her shoulders.

"You look stunning," he announced. "I couldn't take my eyes off you throughout the ceremony."

"You're supposed to look at your sister."

"I've changed her diapers. She'll never charm me with appearances. For the rest of the day, you're mine. I want to hold you dancing. I want to hold you." He nuzzled her neck caused gentle laughter. He possessively led her and Gabe to his car.

"Aren't you driving one of the cars in the wedding procession?"

"I paid my nephew to go in my place in the car. I want to be with you."

During the first slow dance with Brent, Marlo wouldn't her arms around his back and pressed her cheek against his solid muscles. His inviting touch, an occasional brush of his thigh against her hip created shivers of delight. A vision of his warm skin pressed against her nakedness heightened her interest. Luckily, the dance ended and Marlo was able to bring her fantasies under control.

Three line dances in a row with his brothers and sisters and their antics had her sides aching from laughter. Alisha had been right here, too. The wedding and the family's craziness was contagious mayhem. The family included her in their silly antics and jokes. She loved it. If only her days could stay just like this one—happy, fun and overflowing with the warmth of community.

After a wild line dance with two of Brent's brothers, she returned to Brent's side. Perspiration lined her upper lip but Marlo felt more alive than she ever had.

He kissed her forehead. "Hi! You look beautiful—and happy."

"Your family is outrageous." She put her arm around Brent's waist. "But I'm glad I came."

"Me, too. I'll go get us drinks. Wine, or are you willing to try one the bartender's concoctions?"

She glanced over at the bar. Alisha held a reddish fizzing drink. "Ask Alisha what she's having. Ask the bartender if he can create a thirst-quenching nonalcoholic drink. I'll fade away if he makes one of those things I saw him pass to Ian. "

"Ian feels nothing. His eyes are only on Ericka."

"I need to check on Gabe while you get drinks."

Brent watched her retreating figure. Even with Tony gone, she was still uneasy and always wary. She still guarded Gabe. Eventually, he hoped she would let down her vigilance and enjoy life. He wanted time with her alone, time to enjoy together, but he had no idea how to accomplish that task. Maybe at home.

"Hi," he greeted Alisha. "Which of the brothers is buying poor Ian all those drinks?" He gave the bartender his orders.

Alisha leaned on the bar before her. "Everyone is buying for poor Ian. You seem to be enjoying the wedding. Any plans?"

Brent swirled the liquid in his before him. "Plans? For what?" He knew what his sister hinted about, but he wasn't willing to answer. Actually, he wasn't sure what he'd answer. Marlo occupied a special part of his life, a special part of his heart which no one had ever held. He wasn't sure he wanted to share that discovery.

"You seem pretty serious about her. " Alisha smoothed the front of her dress and lowered her tone.

"And you aren't curious?"

Brent shook his head.

"I've watched the looks between you. You want her close to touch. She blushes at every mention of your name. Things are developing quickly."

"I can handle this without family interference."

"You're an O'Neill, You don't get a life without family interference." She poked him in the arm with each word. "You've helped each of us find the 'proper' mate. If you think we're not going to interfere, you are delusional. "

"So what are you two so seriously discussing?" Cameron ordered drinks and stood between Alisha and Brent.

"Brent and Marlo and his next move."

"Now that you've bedded her, your next move should be onward to another woman. Even after Tony, there are still some mysteries unsolved about this woman. With all your contacts, have you investigated more about her?" Cameron gulped his drink.

"No, I know some things from the investigation after Tony's

death."

"Aren't you curious?" Cameron faced his brother.

Brent shook his head.

"When are you going to get curious?" Cameron pushed his point.

"One of the things Marlo needs, one of the things I'm trying to develop between the two of us is trust. I'll trust her to tell me what I need to know when the time comes." He drank his wine in one gulp.

Alisha cautiously sipped her drink. "We all like her. She's fun, willing to put up with us, a good mother … and she certainly has your attention. We like that you have an interest."

"My advice is get away from her before you get in bigger trouble. She's blinded your good judgment."

Brent's fist tightened around his glass. Alisha moved to separate her brothers. "Come on, Cameron, before Brent breaks your thick skull and mops the floor with you." She tapped Cameron on the hand with her fingernail. "The rest of us like her. We like what we've seen. Brent trusts her." She rested her other hand on the tense arm of Brent. "You open your eyes, Cameron. Redeem yourself in your brother's eyes and be the gracious brother and ask Marlo to dance. *Now*, Cameron." She pointed to Marlo walking across the floor.

"Now why should I dance with her? I don't like or trust her." He ordered his next drink.

"I'm the older sister. I hate it when you fight and Brent deserves to hit you. Go." She shoved the edge of Cameron's arm.

"Dance with me and stop a family feud." Cameron stepped in front of Marlo.

"You said something about me, didn't you?" She glanced over at the florid face of Brent who still clenched his glass.

Cameron took her hand in his and limply placed a hand at her waist and moved away from Brent. "What do you want from Brent? Marriage get you out of a jam? A rich man to care for you? He's not loaded, but his property and his honor are worth something."

"Nothing. I didn't ask for anything from Brent. I told you, we moved her to start over. Brent was helpful. I'm not looking for marriage and Brent isn't proposing." She rested her hand on Cameron's shoulder and smiled widely at Brent. Cameron moved into the middle of the floor and away from Brent's glare.

"Yet. He hasn't asked."

Marlo stopped. Others moved around them. "No, Cameron I'm not marrying your brother. I'm not the right woman for him."

Cameron turned her and floated across the floor toward the bar. "Make sure you tell him that. He's falling in love with you." Cameron let go of her hand and turned her gracefully into Brent's waiting arms.

"Hi." Brent took her out stretched hand and pulled her to him at the oak bar. "Did I tell you how that dress catches my eye every time you whirl past?" His mouth grazed her earlobe. "I have the most beautiful woman here accompanying me. Good thing Cameron didn't dance long."

Alisha had a Cheshire cat grin as she poked Marlo's arm. "Sometimes it pays to take care of yourself. Spend a little time and money on yourself and not just care for Gabe. Nice dress." She moved off to join her husband on the dance floor.

"What was that about?" Brent asked.

"Sometimes your siblings confuse me." To herself, she could admit, Alisha had been right. Dressing up, finding a dress that brought admiring glances created a self-confidence she didn't know she could have.

"Get used to it. I've always lived with them and they still confuse me. Here's your drink. How was Gabe?"

"Playing a modern version of Blind Man's Bluff." She positioned herself on the bar stool and straightened her dress.

"Didn't know you haven't been right there with him, did he?"

"No." She sipped her drink. "I'm letting him go, giving him his own space. It's hard. I protected him so long."

"Alisha's right. Sometimes you need to take care of your needs, too. Gabe shouldn't always be first. It has been such a difficult time for both of you. You need to try things you enjoy. What did you and Cameron talk about? He was civil, wasn't he?"

Marlo felt the blush rush up her neck to her face. She stared at her toes tapping on the stool rung. "He was fine. Cameron was himself." Suspicious, too close to the truth, unforgiving after Tony. All the things he had every right to be. But she couldn't share that with Brent. "Your family has been so open. So sharing."

Brent stood closer and teased the back of her neck with his fingers. "They like you. You earned their respect. I told you wouldn't be a stranger long in Trenton." He blew little circles along her hairline, which caused tingles up and down her spine. "Come on. Let's sneak away from my family's watchful eyes. I want you to myself."

Brent held her hand and led her behind curtains near the window. He placed the drinks on the nearby window sill. "I've wanted you to myself all morning." He caressed her shoulders, her neck, her earlobes with feathery kissed, and then his mouth captured hers in a sizzling kiss. She kissed him with a hunger and flicked her tongue along the inside of his lips. He drew her body to his. His hardness pressed against her pelvis indicated the corner was not enough.

He leaned back. His gaze also caressed her. "It's all I can do to keep my hands off you. You invade my thoughts all day. I fantasize about you lying in the bed my arms around you. This time, Gabe will be in another room."

Her heart pounded at his words echoed her own sentiments.

"I want you in my bed, my arms, Marlo Saunders. I want to bring out cries of passions, feel your hands, feel you beneath me."

She put her fingers on his lips. His words sparked a flame deep within her. "I want to be with you. Images of the picnic, the feel of you beneath my fingers haunts me."

"What are we going to do about these desires?"

Before she responded, Cameron threw back the curtain. "I've been called upon to find you. Ceremonies."

Brent led Marlo out on the floor where a group of females clustered. When Marlo saw the flowers in Ericka's hands, she tried to escape, but was pinned in by O'Neill relatives.

"Throw it, Ericka!" the crowd yelled around her. The

flowers flew in Marlo's direction. As if watching a slow motion video, she watched them descending toward her. Marlo didn't lift her hands. Alisha bumped into her. As she raised her hands for balance, the flowers dropped there. The crowd whooped and swung her around to the waiting victim of the garter toss. Brent waited holding the garter. Thrust into the center of the group amid catcalls and advice, she sat her leg out for Brent to place the garter.

"Higher, Brent, we want flashes of that leg to thrill us in our married lives," came cries from the edge of the circle.

"Why do I feel we were set up?" Brent asked as he knelt before her.

Feeling his finger on her inner leg, she held her breath. His fingers glided slowly up her thigh caused her knees to quiver. This was not a moment she wanted to share with an audience.

"Come on, Brent, keep going."

She could barely breathe as his fingers brushed against her inner thigh, higher. She knew he could see up her dress.

"Garters?" he whispered. "So sensual. I have vivid fantasies about garters."

"Keep going," his brothers yelled. "We want more."

"That's for my eyes only."

A boisterous protest followed Brent's remark.

The final dance included children and she and Brent linked hands with Gabe and waltzed around.

"Mommy, can I ride home with Aunt Alisha and Jason? Max is, too. We have games to play in the car and they have awesome DVDs."

She was surprised at his awesome DVD comments. Gabe considered her grin an agreement, and jumped up and down still holding their hands.

"Good." Brent released Gabe who ran to Jason's side. Brent still held Marlo's hand. "I want you to myself on the ride home and if he's with Alisha, I'll take his spot with you."

Alisha confirmed Gabe's invitation. "In case we're separated on the way or you take longer." She nodded to her brother. "I'll keep Gabe at my house until you get there. I have my cell phone if you need to check on him."

Brent took her keys and put his bags in the car on top of

hers and Gabe's. Gabe waved as the van left. Traffic snarled separating them from Alisha. Brent and Marlo sang oldies with the radio as the background and laughed at each other. Marlo felt as if she floated on the air.

She didn't even see the approaching car until it hit sending the car spinning. Brent fought the wheel until and finally brought it under control under the branches of the tree inches from the tree trunk.

The police quickly converged to check on the car. Other than a dent in the car door, Marlo saw no apparent damage. Once the other driver answered the police questioning, he quickly disappeared.

"You, okay?" Brent studied her face.

"Shook up, but no real problems, I think. You? That was some driving?"

"I'm okay. Though it would be much worse. " He conferred with the policeman and they examined the car. Brent returned several minutes later. "The oil pan's leaking and some evidence we lost brake fluid. We ran over a rotting tree trunk that did some damage. You ride in the police car. I'll go with the tow truck. We're going to the nearest garage. Once we're checked out, we can go home. I'll call Alisha on the cell phone from there."

Marlo waited glancing out at her car through the picture window of a body shop. Brent looked under the car with the serviceman. Marlo chewed gum to quiet her nerves. She knew little about cars and was glad Brent was with her not Gabe. Brent came back.

"You sure you're okay?"

"Just bruised and shook up. You?"

"Angry more that anything. Driver was an idiot. I reached Alisha. She has the boys and they are fine and will be glad to keep Gabe."

"Until?"

"Until the car is repaired. The front end is damaged."

"How long? How much damage?" She tried to keep the note of panic out of her voice.

"Don't know yet." He avoided eye contact. "Depends on what parts they have. Maybe we'll have to stay the night."

She watched his face. The night. No Gabe. A night with Brent. What was Brent thinking?

"Want any soda, coffee?" He jingled the change in his pocket, but still did not look at her.

"When will you know? What do you want to do?" She finally voiced her questions.

His blue eyes searched her face for clues. His heart raced. He knew exactly what he wanted, but would she? Gabe was far away. They were alone for the first time in a long time.

"We'll know soon. I—" He sat and she moved beside him. He touched her sleeve, and then put his hands on his knees. He felt like teenager on a date. He wanted her. Wanted to touch her in all the ways he had imagined in the past month. He wanted to feel her beneath him and wanted to wipe out every fear if only for just one night.

"Yes, me too," she said.

He glanced up. His chest pounded. She understood what he was thinking? She wanted a night, too?

"I don't know what to wish for. No damage or an excuse for an overnight. *Together*," he added. He held her hand. Her fingers were ice cold, but a tentative smile played across her lips.

After a pause, she stated, "Yes. Brent."

His calloused thumb stroked her palm. "Good. I have been picturing a sensuous, romantic seduction scene all afternoon."

"So you hit the car or willed it to fly across the intersection to bring about a fantasy?" Her head tilted as she studied his face.

He laughed. He brought her fingers up to his lips and kissed each tip. "Not even for a fantasy would I will an accident. Fate has rolled a chance. A welcome time together. I want you in my arms tonight, Marlo Saunders."

She nodded and squeezed his fingers.

The mechanic returned with the verdict. The best he could promise was early the next morning.

Brent made a few phone calls searching for a motel. A nearby race track with a large purse race had booked all hotel rooms.

For a moment, he worried they would have to call an O'Neill

to come rescue them and drive them home. But he found a small motel off the beaten path.

Chapter Ten

Once inside the motel room, Marlo glanced at the trappings. A dull multi-striped bedspread stretched across the double bed. Matching curtains shut out all light. The wall had a dark abstract painting in the middle across from the bed. It did little to cheer the toneless room.

The room was clean. Basic. Clean, but well, clean was a factor. She didn't budge from her spot near the door. A cheap roadside motel room for a wild tryst. The flat taste in her mouth and the tightness in her stomach had replaced her anticipation in the garage. She wanted Brent. Wanted to freely touch and explore all of him. Wanted to see if she could create the sounds of pleasure from him that he had elicited from her on the picnic. Wanted that same roller coaster feeling she'd had on the picnic. But standing in the doorway of a cheap motel room doused her courage and her desire. She turned to go, when Brent walked in. He, too, stopped in the doorway and viewed the room.

"Not my fantasy for a sensual evening. A little gentler, better room … " He hesitated. The expression on his face mirrored her own disappointment in the room. But he was here. She wanted to touch the hairs curling out of his collar. She wanted to lean against his naked chest. It wouldn't matter what trappings decorated the room. All she needed was Brent.

"No, it's fine." She didn't want to be anywhere but here with him. Brent's eagerness to be together had been visible in the shop. She didn't want to complain about faded wallpaper or faded colors and ruin their time.

"Why don't you take a hot bath while I unload our bags?" He nestled her next to his chest and rested his chin on her head. "You've been jostled in the car and a bath may help." He hesitated. "You okay with this?"

Marlo wasn't' sure if he referred to the bath, the accident of what they both wanted in this room. She nodded against the contours of his chest. "I'm fine with all this, Brent. I'm ready, or will be after a bath." She moved away from his embrace.

He leaned down as if to kiss her, then moved to the door. "Let me finish with business. I'll be back … soon."

Marlo sunk into the hot water and pushed a button that shot jets onto a body. The whirl and bump of the car in the accident slipped into her thoughts. But the swirling waters of bathtub Jacuzzi relaxed her muscles. She soaped her washcloth and swirled it around her breasts and down the front of her belly. Soon she would feel Brent's hands.

She would be able to explore his body. She had watched his body move, run in races, bend over to help Gabe. With each movement, she had wanted to run her fingers over the chest muscles, hold that body close to hers and explore parts she only thought of in her fantasies. Memories of the picnic and the peaks he had enticed in her also tantalized her memories. Soon she would touch, explore and discover if she were able to unleash Brent's passions with her explorations. She ducked further into the water, letting the scent and feel of the bath envelop her senses.

She rubbed down her body with the soft towel. She picked out jeans, a T-shirt and the lacy bra and panties from her suitcase that Brent had already dropped in their room. Once she was behind the bathroom door, she reached for the black lacy bra she and Alisha had chosen on their shopping spree. Her image in the bathroom full-length mirror captured her attention.

Who was that woman with the slight smile who anticipated lovemaking, who wanted to fill the room cries of passion—both his and hers? Certainly not the same woman who had been at Tony's beck and call. She unfastened her bra and flung it aside. She tossed aside the matching lace panties. She shrugged into her jeans and pulled a T-shirt over her bare chest. She sat on the bed until Brent returned.

Brent hesitated at the door, his hands full of his bag and her small case. He swallowed. "Feel better after your bath?" His voice came out as a hoarse whisper.

The very air around Marlo seemed electrified. Her pulse pounded. Her excitement motivated her. She closed the door behind him. Rising on her toes, she kissed with a hunger and passion that matched the heat building inside. Then she kissed him again, demanding more. Brent dropped the suitcases and his hands encircled her face.

Her fingers fumbled with button on his shirt. She abandoned the kiss to undo his shirt and reach the dark curls she had longed to touch since the wedding. She pushed aside the front of his shirt and placed a palm on his chest. "You'll have to tell me what you like."

"Touch me. Your touch is wonderful," came out as a low moan as she played with skin across his shoulders then moved down the center of his chest. "Touch me wherever."

Her fingers roved across his pecs, she rolled his nipple between her thumb and forefinger, which elicited another sound deep from within his chest. She watched his eyes darken as she ran her nails down the length of his abs and across the bulge of expanding denim.

His hands slipped beneath her T-shirt. When he discovered her nakedness beneath, a slow smile crossed his lips. His hands roamed over one breast, then another. Marlo felt as though her body slipped into another realm, a voracious hunger—a hunger only Brent could satisfy.

She pushed his shirt off Brent's shoulders and tugged his jeans to the floor. She ran her index finger the length of him.

"Marlo, I can't wait." He swept her up in his arms and carried her to the bed. He quickly discarded her jersey and jeans. His gaze travelled from her face and down the expanse of her body. She felt desired. One hand slid down her belly to the apex of her curls. Her body, by its own volition, arched toward him. He knelt on the bed and explored her wet folds with his finger. Her body craved his touch. She wanted him inside her satisfying the need that overtook her. "Brent, now, please."

As if he read her mind, Brent stretched for his shirt lying crumbled on the floor and took a condom from the pocket.

Her need for him was almost unbearable. She rocked her

hips in a motion to relieve some of the tension spiraling inside. She moved with him. A rush of pleasure coursed through her with each thrust of his hips. Their bodies deepened the thrusts, quickened the rhythms. Every sensation in her entire body seemed focused on one spot. She tossed her head back and forth. Time spiraled out of control. The only moment was then and the feel of him within her. Waves of passion seared through her body. Then an explosion of sensations overtook every fiber of her being.

Tiny aftershocks coursed through her. She felt as though she were slowly floating down from the ceiling. Brent's head rested on her shoulder, soft sounds of his breathing tickled her ear.

"Are you alright? I wanted you so much."

She kissed his shoulder. Her hands caressed his back. She was incapable of any sound, any words. Brent rolled to his side next to her. His hand roamed down her side.

"I've never been like that. Never felt like that making love."

Brent played with her hair. I'm not ready to move for a while. I'd just like to hold you."

She moved closer and settled in firmness of his embrace. His embrace grounded her. She closed her eyes and savored the sensations of completeness, the warmth of him beside her. He stretched his arm across her belly.

"What are you thinking?" He reached over her body for her hand. She rolled her over until their bodies aligned. Her hands stroked his chest. At night before she dozed off, she thought of the hairs on his chest and her need to run her fingers across his chest. He felt much better than any of her imaginings.

"I like touching you. I can't stop."

"No one's complaining."

"After, I just want to touch, stroke, feel you beneath my fingers. You feel so good." "Good" seemed to be a weak term to describe the taut muscles and the soft hairs as she glided her fingers across his chest.

He wiggled his shoulders until he lay flat on his back, and guided her down until her head nestled on his arm. Her hand still rubbed his chest. He kissed the top of her head. "I could stay like this for a long time. You feel right in my arms. I've thought about what you would sound like, feel like deep inside."

She snuggled closer and enjoyed the closeness. Both were quiet. She, too, could last like this. She sighed deeply and moved her chin against his side.

"So why did you run from me? Hide with Miriam?"

She paused. She had intimately shared herself with him, now was a time to share her thoughts as well. "I'd always followed another's opinion, other people's orders for too long. I need to make decisions for myself."

"I wouldn't have been in your way. I would honor your independence." His hand roamed down her side.

"It would have been easy to go to you and let you deal with the investigation. But my past, what I had done, why I had been involved with Tony and why I had run to Maine … I didn't think you'd understand my feelings. I didn't know if you'd want to see me again." Once she had stated it, her statement was ludicrous. He, of all people, understood her better than anyone. "My relationship with Tony wasn't open. I couldn't discuss with Tony. It was his way."

"He hit you that day. He had before."

She swallowed. Brent certainly cut to the chase. Could she let him know her past? She had hidden it so long and even accepted it as her error and her terror. "A husband's prerogative was to hit, Tony said. He had a temper. Violence was a response. When I was there, with him, I never saw it any differently."

"Miriam said you married young."

"I was seventeen when I met him. I had little experience with men … with life. He was a way out."

He stroked her arm to give support. "Out?"

She closed her eyes. Memories she had tried to escape, tried to drive away as if they weren't part of her today, swept back with a rush with the impact of a fast moving storm. She paused, drew a deep breath. "You might as well know it all. My parents died when I was ten. My aunt and uncle raised me. Their children were grown and gone, so to them I was a burden. A responsibility."

He kissed her temple. "A loss at a young age. Any siblings?

Any memories of your parents?" The arm around her shoulders tightened in a squeeze.

"Yes, happy ones. Two loving parents. Caring, touching, laughing. Ideal marriage. Or maybe those are just memories I glorified so I could survive the coldness at my aunt's. My brother and I were adopted by different relatives. I haven't seen him since I was ten." As if she had moved to a different realm, Marlo's voice changed to a low strained tone. Her body tightened within his arms.

"Tough times. Confusing and no one to talk with." He voiced the concerns. He could understand her reluctance to share with him. Her fears of being close. "When you met Tony—"

"I was a young clerk. I was very plain, and just breaking into adolescence. I was confused. Unsure. He took me places and dazzled me with his wealth, knowledge, sophistication."

Her stroking of him had stopped. Her hands rested on his chest. A striking tension had all her muscles tied in knots.

"I saw none of the Tony's evils. Maybe I wouldn't have known then. Maybe I wanted to be blind." Her chin sank lowered.

Brent had to strain to hear her.

"What? Keep talking. There's a tragedy somewhere you're not saying. I won't judge you. I want to help. Talk to me." He pushed himself up on his elbow.

Marlo lay on her back looking up at him. Her eyes were flat, gone was the animation he had just witnessed moments before. She stared at a spot beyond him. "Tell me." He kissed her forehead and stroked the length of her forearm. She appeared unaware of his touch.

"What happened? What nightmare are you carrying?"

She closed her eyes and shook her head as if driving off an image deep within her mind. Her face tensed as if her teeth clenched an object in her mouth. He waited.

Finally, she continued, "Tony was violent."

"You didn't deserve any of that. Whatever he did you weren't responsible for that."

"No." She held up her hand to stop him and to clear the image before her. "I shouldn't have left him. It was my fault.

Tony never let me out without him accompanying me." Her voice faltered. "Someone had to stay with the baby." She stopped.

"Gabe is okay now. Whatever happened in the past …"

"No, the baby before Gabe." Her facial expression changed almost as if she were somewhere else. A different Marlo appeared before him. She was unaware of his presence. She was someone in the past describing terrors of that past.

"He had two men there, two men discussing some plan. They swore it was an accident. I knew …" She stopped.

Brent waited. Her face twisted in anguish. He stroked her jaw line. "Marlo," he said softly. "You were away, what happened, you couldn't have prevented."

"I went shopping. I had never gone without him before. After the pregnancy, I needed clothes. I shouldn't have gone out. I shouldn't have left him." Her words tumbled out. "Tony was in a meeting with the men. The baby asleep. Then I must have stayed out too long. The baby wouldn't stop crying …"

Brent brought her back within the fold of his arms. When her last words came out, she was buried in his arms.

"The baby was dead by the time I got there. Tony had SIDS written down. It wasn't SIDS." The last came out in angry bitterness. "The baby didn't instantly obey."

Brent swallowed the bile building in his throat. The life she had survived.

"Did you leave?"

"Not then. I moved in a grieving haze. Tony flooded me with gifts, trips. He made it seem right somehow. For a year, he overwhelmed me with kindness." Her fingers clutched the bed sheet behind them. Her body was rigid within his arms.

"Then I had Gabe. Gabe was the security Tony needed. I feared for Gabe. I saved nickels and dimes for two years. Tony wouldn't notice them. Saved enough for two train tickets. I was picked up by two of Tony's henchmen before I got two towns away."

She finally looked at Brent. "He said he'd kill Gabe before my eyes if I ever tried again."

"What happened? How did you get away?" He wanted to keep her talking. Get her to the point she relaxed, to a point she would come back to the present.

"I couldn't risk Gabe. Then the FBI made it easy. They were after Tony. Tony was initially picked up on a simple vehicle tie-up on the interstate. Police held him, then Miriam talked with me." Part of the tension eased from her body. Her voice remained flat and monotone. "The decision was easy. I knew little, but it helped them. They helped me relocate to a quiet area. Maine."

He couldn't find the appropriate response. Her trust, innocence and integrity had been destroyed. Toughness, single-mindedness, silence had been her survival traits.

"I don't know what beam of magic led you to Trenton, but I'm grateful you came. I've never met anyone like you." He cupped her cheek in his hand. What hell this woman had been through, yet she kept a goodness, a hopefulness, an eagerness about life. Brent close his eyes. So much pain. As she expressed her horrors, she looked as if she had been gouged with a sharp blade. No wonder she protected Gabe. What would it take to erase these memories and replace them with laughter and fun?

She started to back out of his arms. "I don't fit with Trenton's families. My life has little goodness. I don't know that I can ever fit in. Your family —" The words caught in her throat and she stopped as if trying revive choked words from deep within. "I'm not like you or your family. I don't know how to do so much. I don't want to disgrace your family."

"Disgrace my family? You honor us by being with us. Such a tough woman to stand up to so much." He kissed her forehead. "If I could erase any of that for you ... You're a remarkable woman."

She tensed again and pushed away from him with her palms. He didn't release her from his grasp. "Brent, I was a criminal's wife. Things went on, I shouldn't have been so blind, so childlike and so pliant. I was a criminal's wife." She emphatically spat out the last five words.

"Tony was a criminal. You were courageous and honest ... and trusting. You're out of your nightmare." He stoked the back of her head and pulled her closer. "I am grateful you came. You are a gift."

His arms wrapped around her naked back. Her chest crushed against his. His strength was invigorating. Their talk was cleansing.

She breathed in deeply. "I've never shared that with anyone. I talk with you, in a way I never do."

"I know." His kisses started the top of her head and worked down to her collarbone. He paused. "You are a survivor, a fighter woman, Marlo Saunders. Just incredible." With his words ringing in her ears and the warmth of his body tightly closed around her, she fell asleep.

He held her close to him. He couldn't erase any of her memories. This astonishing woman in his arms had braved a bitter childhood and terrifying marriage to a violent, controlling man yet remained a positive, forceful woman. She kept herself under such tight control. Would he ever be able to break through the fortress that had been her survival? Formidable task.

He liked the feel of her next to him. The soft rise and fall of the steady breathing next to his chest was reassuring. Since he sat next to Marlo in Tillie's, his life had changed.

•

Awakening in a darkened room, the warmth of Brent's body and the feel of his arm draped across her brought her quickly to her senses. The warm security of his arms made her feel alive.

"Good morning." He rubbed her back between her shoulders. She understood why cats purred; this was heavenly. He slid his hand down her backbone. Tingles followed his touch.

The phone rang. Marlo jumped. Brent's reassuring hand touched her shoulder. He reached for the phone

"It was just the shop. The car is almost ready." Brent slid out of the bed and in unabashed nakedness walked to the other side of the bed. The phone still hung in his hand. "Did the phone waken you?"

"I've had phone call at home." She picked at the top of the sheet. "Just hangs up. Breathing. Little talk."

Brent scowled. "Probably kids." He placed the phone in the receiver. He sat on the bed beside her. "Or a wrong number.

Anyone say anything or ask for anything?"

"A male voice said, 'Marlo DeFalco.'" She pulled the covers to her chin.

He held her fingers in between his palms. "Tony's dead. Whomever is calling, it's a mistake. Your terrible past is done." He stretched out next to her. The thin sheet separated his nakedness from hers. He wrapped his fingers around her hair hanging down her shoulder. "You're safe in Trenton. I'm there for you. We can investigate the calls just so you know you are safe."

She gazed into his eyes. "The feeling won't go away. The feeling that kept Gabe and me alive. A warning when something was wrong. I can't shake it."

"You'll learn to let down that guard now. Tony's gone. You will relax, let go of those fears. Trenton is the place."

Brent studied her face. He wanted the moment to last. He wasn't ready to go home. But both had duties in the real world. His job, her child. He wanted her to associate their time with good memories not the anguish of confessing past frights. "Come on, shower time"

"A shower?" She repeated as he led her from the bed to the bathroom. He turned on shower and found motel soap, shampoo.

His wolfish grin disarmed her. "It's the least I can do after last night is soap down every body part I can reach. Tangle my fingers in your hair." He stretched a dry curl around his finger. "Your long hair, every tantalizing strand of it, when it brushes against my chest, piques my interest." He ran his fingers through her hair.

They entered the shower. He soaped her shoulders, her arms. Slowly he soaped her neutral and warm zones stoically avoiding her most intimate areas.

Her hands fingered his chest hairs, she floated her long hair against his shoulders, her breasts teased his chest. The enticing time begun yesterday continued.

"I could stay here and keep this shower, this time going." She relaxed. Nothing in her previous life compared to this.

"I don't want you to leave, Marlo Katherine Saunders."

She leaned into him, the water beat down on the both of

them.

"Marry me, Marlo."

"What?" She jumped back.

He didn't move. The soap and sponge remained in his hands. "Marry me." The blue eyes steadily looked at her searching her thoughts.

She swallowed. Her breath came in slow gasps as if someone had placed a towel over her head. Her arms stretched to the shower walls to brace herself. She couldn't think clearly, couldn't breath regularly. Her past crushed her present. Her legs felt weak, her head dizzy.

"I know this isn't the most romantic way to propose. I'll make it up for it when we get home. I love you, Marlo. You've changed my life in ways I can't express." The shower water streamed over his face.

A proposal now. Never could anyone prepare for a shower proposal.

With both his hands wrapped around hers, he led her out of the shower stall and wrapped a towel around her. "Marry me." He wiped the water from her eyes. "Say something. Answer me."

She swallowed. "Brent, I don't … This wasn't anything I expected or thought of." Time stopped. She couldn't move.

He stared at the floor. "I know most people don't propose in showers."

"No, Brent, please." Tears welled in her eyes. This should be a glorious time. A proposal. "No, Brent I can't …"

"You can't? I don't understand you. You told me this was your most incredible weekend. You said you've never been this way. I want this to last, Marlo. What we have together is incredible. I want to be this way forever."

She shook her head.

He stared at her. She couldn't meet his gaze. What could she say? He wanted her more that a one-night fling. She certainly wanted him. He was more than anyone could ever make up in a fantasy. But she couldn't. Not yet.

He placed a towel around his waist staggered out of the bathroom. She turned off the shower, towel dried her hair as she tried to get her emotions under control. She wanted him, trusted him, but she couldn't marry him. Not now. She wasn't sure she knew how to explain her feelings.

Brent, clad only in jockey shorts, stood before the window. Silent, stoic and staring out the window. What could she possibly say to make it any better? She walked over to him, lifted her hand to touch him, then turned and walked across the room to the opposite side of the bed.

"I don't know how to explain, Brent. It's not reason, it's … You are the best thing to ever happen in my life."

"But you're not willing to commit."

"Brent." A deep sigh moved through Brent's body, but he still stared out the window. She was probably better if she didn't have to look him in the eye. "So much has changed in my life. I have no idea who I am. You have helped me so much, not just with the cottage, but you're caring, unconditionally accepting me. Loving me." The last two words trailed off to almost a whisper. "I am grateful."

"Grateful!" Brent exploded.

She automatically flinched.

He stared at her as if she were a stranger—a stranger he didn't want to know. His posture was rigid. His blue eyes unflinching.

Marlo sighed, feeling the sadness seeping throughout her body to the depth of her toes. She stared at a rust colored piece of lint. Silence crackled in the room.

She walked to the window, reached to touch Brent's shoulder, then let her hands fall to her sides. "Brent. Please try to understand. My emotions are running in contradictory directions. I've spent my whole life keeping myself in line. Now I feel deeply. Is that love?" She pleaded her case to his back. She didn't want to lose him in her life, but she couldn't commit to a lifetime. Not yet. "I'm trying to discover the Marlo inside. How can I trust myself on anything?"

"Trust, again." Rancor sharpened his tone.

"I'm frightened."

"I'm not Tony," he stated before she could add anything.

"No, I'm not afraid of you." She touched his shoulder. "I love the time with you. I love the games, your family, the dates." She averted her face and said quietly, "I certainly love the physical relationship, but I can't promise you a lifetime, yet."

"Yet." He sketched a pattern on the window with his finger.

"It's not over. The dangers …"

Brent turned and clutched her shoulders tightly in his hands. "Tony's dead. That life is over. You're safe in Trenton. I'll protect you from your fears." His clipped tone revealed the pain he was in.

"Something isn't right. I keep waiting for the other shoe to fall." She struggled to find the right words. "Something evil is right around the corner."

His dark eyes showed his bafflement. His grip never lessened.

"My aunt's expression. One thing happens and you just know the rest is to follow. One shoe falls, you wait for the sound of the other. I can't shrug off the nagging sense of doom. I wait for someone to show up at my door. Any boat pausing in the water near the house is a cause for worry. The phone calls." She faltered. She couldn't explain it logically to herself, how could she ever get him to understand?

"You reject me for a sense." Unthinking, he shook her. His frown deepened.

"My sense kept me alive, saved Gabe." She shrugged out of his grasp and stepped to the other side of the room. "I can't commit a lifetime to a wonderful man." She faced him. "Until I completely let go of that sense of foreboding and can give one hundred percent to that man."

"This isn't healthy for Gabe or for you to hang onto your fears, to hang on to nightmares of your past. Leave it behind. You can start over in Trenton. Give me a chance to be a part of that future."

"Brent, you are important in my life. Gabe's life."

"This isn't about Gabe. It's about you and me. You are an individual. A woman with your own feelings and a life separate from Gabe. Search with those feelings."

She met his gaze. She said nothing. Sobs congested in her chest. She couldn't cry now.

"Those feelings you exhibited last night were false? Your

response to me in that bed last night was a response to every male?"

"No." She slumped to the nearest chair. "Wanting you, reaching those peaks of need are very real. Talking with you as we did last night was real. You're a gift in my life. A gift I don't know if I deserve."

"You're a caring, passionate woman. Having someone love you is not a crime. You're not an undeserving criminal. You did nothing to help Tony. You didn't kill the baby."

She flinched at his last statement. The tears fell despite her good intentions. "I can't love you the way you need. You deserve a woman who can love you with no holds barred. No worries. I can't give you that."

"Can't or *won't* try."

"Not yet, Brent. Too much has happened for me to give up my sense of foreboding. I'm afraid to love you. I'm afraid I will cause you too much pain."

"This isn't painful?" He returned to his window stance. His fists clenched.

She remained away from him. "I love as best I can, but it's not the love you want."

He faced her. "So now what?"

"I don't know." She pulled her T-shirt over her head and finished dressing. "I don't want to lose you."

"I don't know if I can do that. Seeing you, wanting you, and knowing you're not sure of me is too much."

Her head sunk to her chest.

The phone rang. She didn't move Brent answered. "The car's ready." He walked to the chair, then pulled on his jeans. "I'll get the car while you finish dressing."

He paused at the door. "I love you, Marlo. I won't desert you if you need me. The cottage is yours until you make up your mind. Obviously, we'll see each other in town. Trenton is small. I won't wait forever."

The ride home was interminable and tortuous. Small talk about scenery changes and wedding pictures filled the time. Both avoided personal comments.

Chapter Eleven

"Look, Mom." When they returned, Gabe greeted them at the end of Alisha's lane. He turned his bike and rode away. The bike steady. His fear conquered.

"Oh." Marlo's hand covered her mouth as her son rode away from her, not into her arms. He would start school soon. Their world spun differently. Gabe learned new skills and was free to be a child.

Alisha hugged her. "He's practiced all morning so he could show you that. How was your night?" She looked from her brother back to Marlo. Brent studied the driveway. Marlo looked at Gabe wobbling back on the dirt road.

"Thank you for keeping Gabe last night. My car is fine now," Marlo said. *My heart feels as if someone ran over it instead.* She didn't dare look at Brent.

"I need to report in to work. Check on the things." Brent hesitated by the car. "I'll be in touch." Marlo watched his taillights disappear down the graveled road. She willed herself to breathe steadily and not to cry.

She needed to mask her emotions to face Alisha. Brent was her brother. "Thanks again, Alisha. I had a great time at the wedding."

"Did the wedding help you at all with your idea of marriage?" Alisha asked.

"More than you will know."

"You and Brent had fun. Cameron behaved. Brent couldn't keep his eyes off you with that dress." Alisha kept up her analysis of the wedding. Her hands waved as she described scenes in the wedding. Alisha saw only goodness in the interactions between her and Brent.

"It's always fun to be with your family. Ericka looked radiant." Marlo patted Alisha on the arm and left before she had to answer any more questions.

Marlo sat on the front step watching Gabe pedal up and down the dirt road before the cottage practicing his newfound skill. Gabe would start school in three weeks. Maybe as they slipped into the routine of school and a home, she could concentrate on her new life and let go of the past. She needed a job. Alisha had suggested the local library. With a job, a schedule, she could become Marlo Saunders and discard the fearful, timid Marlo DeFalco. And Brent? She wanted him in her life. Hopefully, he would wait until she could get her life together. She sighed. Tomorrow would have answers. She had to learn to depend on her tomorrows.

With the lingering warmth of the early fall sun beating on her face, she sensed the seasonal changes in the air.

"Gabe, one more time and we go in. It's getting darker earlier. Gabe?" She hadn't heard the tires. Had he fallen off while she was daydreaming?

"Gabe?" She ran to the dirt road. He was nowhere in sight. "Gabe?" She sprinted down the road. His bike lay on its side, the front wheel still spun, the brush around it was broken. "Oh my God." A path of broken twigs led to the shore. "Gabe?" She searched the shore. No signs of him. "Gabe!" she screamed.

Mrs. Carlson shouted from her yard. "What's wrong? What's wrong, Marlo?"

The hairs rose on her neck. She knew the feeling. Ominous. "Call Brent," she yelled. "Gabe's gone. Call the police quick. Get them!" Marlo's heart pounded. Her mouth dried. Silently she prayed, *Please let him be here unharmed.* She raced down the path where she had last seen Gabe. She called his name. No answer.

A Trenton squad car and Brent arrived at the same time. They searched the immediate area.

"Go over the details again." Brent held both her hands in his. The other policeman paused beside them. Another police car arrived.

"I was right here, Brent. On the porch. He was nearby riding his bike. Close enough to protect him. What could have happened? I let him out of my sight for a few minutes." Marlo gripped Brent's hand.

"Okay. You go inside with Alisha. We'll comb the area. Maybe he's just hiding." Gabe hadn't answered any of their calls. Marlo had shown them where she found the bike. They would comb the area.

"Brent, something's wrong, I know it. Do something!" She grabbed his arm. "Please, find him." She whispered the last words.

He peeled her hand off his arm and handed her over to Alisha. "Go inside. Maybe we'll notice something you missed. Alisha, take care of her." He walked back to the crime scene with the other cops and rescue team.

"So what do you really think, Brent?" Franklin of Camden's rescue team questioned. "Sounds really hokey to me. Drowned her own kid. Bet we find him floating."

Was he that gullible? Brent studied the ground in front of him as he attempted to piece together what little clues they had. The other baby died. She had confessed in the motel room. Maybe Tony had tried to rescue Gabe and he had shot him. Could she be that deceitful? Could she have duped him? He wasn't that bad a judge of character. She loved Gabe. He loved her. Could he doubt her?

He looked again through the broken branches, twigs. Signs of a struggle here. A tiny piece of material clung to a lower broken branch. Gabe had been here.

"Brent." Patti Closeman, another Trenton policewoman, walked up. "Mrs. Carlson lives there." She pointed. "She heard a boat idling boat about two hours ago. Thought it odd. Heard a cry."

"At the same time?" he and Franklin asked simultaneously.

"No, a boy's cry. About a half hour ago. The boat left."

"Did she see the boat?" Brent searched the shoreline as he questioned. Where was Gabe?

"No. Didn't look out. She said she heard 'cuz she was moving her plants inside."

"Franklin." He pivoted. "Get the Coast Guard." Parts of Miriam's conversation returned. She had mentioned other dangers and the "seem" and "think" words were too real now.

Would Marlo remember anything? He raced to the cottage. "Marlo, I need your help. Tony have any enemies? Any co-workers?"

Before Marlo could answer, the phone rang.

"Where is he? Who are you?" Marlo's responses to the phone call answered what many questions Brent might have had. He crossed to her side as she cried into the receiver.

Brent grabbed the receiver. The line was dead.

"Brent." Marlo's voice was his shrill and piercing. "A man has Gabe. Something from Tony. He and Tony. He won't let me talk to Gabe."

"Easy." Brent held her shoulders. His cop's instincts fought with his lover needs. He wanted to hold her in his arms and make her fears disappear. But if he really wanted to help, he needed details. "Tell me exactly what he said. Try to remember it word for word."

Marlo gulped air in her lungs. Would this never end? Gabe. She swallowed her panic. She had to remember. "He said he was Tony's partner. Gabe is safe as long as I do exactly what he says."

"What does he want you to do?"

"He said I have numbers. I don't know what he's talking about. He'll call back with instructions. I was to tell no one." She flopped on the couch.

"You had to tell me. You know that." He sat beside her and cradled her in his arms. "We'll get through this. Gabe is alive. We'll find him. I'll set up monitoring on the phone. Trace him."

Unable to be still, she paced leaving Brent on the couch. "He wants something from me or I can't have Gabe. Numbers from Tony."

"What did Tony ever give you?"

"I didn't keep any of Tony's gifts to me. I left only with bare essentials." She closed her eyes to close out surge of panic. What could she have of Tony's? She had destroyed any reminders of him, of any touch in her life.

"Think about Tony. What was important to him? He came here. He wanted something from you." Brent watched her pacing, but didn't get up.

She didn't have the right answers. She had no idea why he had come except to destroy her life and seek revenge on her.

"He wanted Gabe." She sat in the rocker facing Brent. She rocked unsteadily. "Told me to pack Gabe's toys. He said nothing about numbers or anything of belongings. We didn't talk much before you arrived."

Brent held her hands between his. "Anything you had with Tony. Photographs. Does Gabe have anything of Tony's? Stuffed animals? A blanket? The suitcase? Inside the suitcase?" Brent stood and started to the bedroom.

"We bought that on the way. Tony's never seen it. Gabe has no reminders of his father except Tony's baseball cards. Only thing of value he gave to his son. "

"The cards?" Brent said slowly. "Tony knew Gabe has the cards?"

She shrugged. "I suppose so. Tony thought they were such a big deal, he instilled that into Gabe. Gabe was much too young to care about baseball." She stood. "The cards! He made me take them with Gabe even when Gabe was a baby. But Tony couldn't have hidden anything in them. There's no room. They're cards with pictures of baseball players."

"Get them." Brent hovered in the hallway as she searched Gabe's room and returned with two notebooks of baseball cards. She and Brent sat at the kitchen table and studied the books and the cars. No hidden spots existed in any way. No numbers behind the cards—just two notebooks full of baseball cards.

"This never made sense to me. Tony was never a sports fan." Marlo flipped one plastic page back. Faces, poses of baseball players blurred in front of her eyes.

"Wait." Brent held up one card. "I had this card as a kid. I read Tekulve's career because I had his card. He didn't play in the sixties; he wasn't old enough. He played for the Pirates and the Phillies, not the Orioles. This card is a fake. But why?"

He studied the card, then placed it back in the plastic slot and studied the others next to it. "They all look real enough. Wait. This one isn't right either. Schmidt was a Philly, too, but not in the sixties. These two go in order, but they're mistakes. The numbers aren't right either."

Marlo stood behind him and looked at the cards. She'd never been a baseball fan. They were foreign to her.

"The numbers don't match baseball card stats. Some I don't recognize, but Cameron was a real collector. He'll be able to pick out mistakes and changes better than me."

"So what? Baseball cards with mistakes not worth anything. What value could they have for Tony? I don't understand." Marlo stood behind Brent staring at the cards he had identified. This was craziness. They needed to find her son.

"A code here. The numbers are coded and in order of some kind. Cameron can figure out irregularities in the cards. A guy in the detective—a specialist can figure the code."

"Here in these cards?" Marlo held up the book. "This is the key? Tony wanted these?" She swung in a wide circle. Gabe would be freed.

"This is probably why he came. Wanted these, not Gabe." Brent stood beside her, but there was no enthusiasm in his action.

"And this is what this guy wants? We have it?" She danced around the kitchen hugging the books to her chest. "We have it. I can go to him give him this, get Gabe back."

"Marlo, you can't go." He stopped her dance and held her by the shoulders. "This guy may be dangerous. He may not stop with just the books."

"Brent, he promised he wouldn't hurt Gabe if I gave him the books. I'm going, Brent. That's my son." She wrenched away from Brent's grasp.

"Marlo, listen to me." Brent followed her into the den. "We won't put Gabe in danger. I won't have you in danger."

She faced him. "This is my son." She would march over anyone to get to Gabe.

When the phone rang again, Marlo jumped near Brent. He steadied her then nodded to the phone. She carefully picked it up.

"Hi, Beauty, I still think of your soft thighs. Your hand on my cheek."

"Who are you?" She demanded. Her hands shook. She swallowed trying to recover and temper her fears. "Where's Gabe? I want my son."

"Remember New Year's Eve two years ago? You were dressed in that low cut blue dress. My eyes were on you all night. Tony didn't mind his partner getting a little action. I touched you. You were soft. I want to run my hands …"

"Tony never had a partner. You're Leo Harrington. You're not Tony's partner."

"You do remember, don't you, honey?" His voice purred. Marlo grimaced. Her skin crawled just thinking of that New Year's Eve. "Tony never gave you permission for anything. You never were with him."

"No," he said, slowly letting his O's roll. "But Tony's dead. Now I'm in charge. I know about the numbers. Know your numbers, too. Tony and me going share lot of partnerships now that he's not here to stop me. You and me, too, little lady. We're gonna share a lot. I've watched you with that little boy playing on the shore. He means a lot to you. You'll do what I say."

"Where's Gabe? Please, can I talk with him so I know he is okay?"

"Did you find me the numbers like I told you?"

"Yes, please let me talk to Gabe."

"You'll just have to trust me with him. Decided to come through, did you? I'll call you soon with directions. No one else must know or you'll never see Gabe again. I don't want that cop in this. The one who wanted you and would have had you on that boat if I hadn't interrupted you. No one else will have you, but me. Remember that." He clicked off.

Marlo stared at the phone in disbelief. "He just hung up," she whispered. "Like that. No Gabe."

"We'll find him." He rubbed her shoulders. "We will."

"He said no one must know. Not you. He mentioned you. You can't help me." She looked at Brent's face. How could he know how important this was?

He placed one hand on each of her shoulders. "Listen. There're ways to deal with this."

She grabbed Brent's shirt at his elbows. "I just want Gabe, Brent, I don't care about trapping this man. I don't care if he gets the numbers. I just need Gabe." To emphasize each point, she shook Brent's shirt. He held steady.

"I won't let anything happen to Gabe. I don't want anything to happen to you, either."

She hung onto his hands as they rested on top of her shoulders. Brent who taught Gabe to fish, to jump into the water wouldn't let anything happen to Gabe. Gabe loved him. She needed him, she needed his support as Brent, the police chief. "Brent, I'm frightened. What if we—"

"We can do this. It means you must be a good actress and trust me to do the rest." He flinched at his word chose as soon as "trust" jumped out of his mouth.

"It's my son."

"Yes, we need your input. The local police, other departments can be called in. We can do an all-out canvass. Someone will be here twenty-four hours until you hear from him. We're all trained for this. Gabe will be alright. I want to hear his plans, too. I'm staying here with you, until this is over." He slipped her hands around his shoulders and held her close. "I want to be here with you until this is over."

She took the comfort his hug offered. She had someone she could trust. They would all have to wait until Harrington's next move.

No phone call came that evening. She slept curled in the security of Brent's arms.

The next day she waited trying to keep busy and near the phone. Brent very rarely left her side.

The next night arrived. Marlo's movements were wooden, her mind numb. Brent unfastened her shirt, warmed lotion in his hands and massaged her back.

"Brent, why didn't he call? Is Gabe dead? Did he feel I wouldn't come through?" She slumped over. Although she was aware of Brent's touch, it seemed distant and didn't help her distraught nerves.

"Wear-down tactics. If he worries you enough, you'll agree to any conditions." He massaged her shoulders.

"It's working. Whatever he wants. As long as I get Gabe back." She rolled over and faced him. "I don't know if he's alive. I've got the cards. We know nothing."

"Gabe is his gambling tool." Brent paced before her. Although he had tried to appear calm to her, his restlessness gave him away. "Without him, no bargaining unit. But we have to be ready to jump in as soon as you exchange the numbers. You and Gabe are disposable then."

Brent studied her. "This man may know a great deal about you and certainly your relationship with Gabe. We don't know how long he spied on you and how much he knows. We've installed separate phone lines so we can listen in on conversations."

"Brent," she said finally. "I want to be a part of decision-making. It's my son. It's my life."

He tightened his hold around her. "We will get Gabe back safely. I believe that." His arms encircled her in the safe cradle of his embrace. He quietly added. "There's a *we*, Marlo Saunders. We will do this together."

The call came two days later.

Chapter Twelve

"So Marlo, how is that scrumptious body of yours? I can't wait to see it again. To see you. More of you." His voice made Marlo's skin crawl.

"Where are you? Where's Gabe?"

"Right here. Say hi, kid."

"Mommy." Gabe's high pitched squeal made her chew on her cuticle.

"Hi, Gabe, it's Mommy. We'll get you."

"We nothing, " Harrington's voice returned. "You and only you will meet me on the Yankee Trader, a whale and puffin watch boat, at two PM."

She glanced at Brent who shook his head and pointed to his watch.

"That's not enough time," she amended. "I can't be sure I can get on at two today. The whale watches are usually reserved days in advance. What if I can't get on? I need a day or two to be sure." She held her breath. Judging from Brent's behavior, he needed time to help rescue Gabe. She was bargaining with Gabe's life. She wanted to meet this guy now. Would he fall for her ploy for time?

Harrington paused. She bit her lip. *Come on.*

"Tuesday. That's the last offer. No stalling," he growled on the other end.

She checked with Brent in the kitchen. His face reflected in the pots hanging above him. Visible lines of worry did not reassure her. The stillness in the room reverberated around her. Brent nodded.

"No one else on board," Harrington demanded. "Not FBI, not friends, not police. I have pictures of all the cops in Trenton.

I'll know if they're on board. I'll drown your boy right in front of you if you don't follow orders."

"How will I know you? Will Gabe be with you?"

"My plans are mine. You'll know me, sweetheart. You'll give me a little present before we part."

"I have the book."

"You wouldn't see Gabe without it. The present I want is a little of you. I remember your breasts in that tight little dress on New Year's Eve. Just enough to fill a man's hand. I want you to fill my hands. I want to fill you. Feel you squirm beneath me."

"I want Gabe before you get this book." She didn't comment on his other demands.

"Two PM on Tuesday. No one else with you. You have the book." The phone clicked in her ear.

Marlo sat holding the phone in her hand looking at the receiver. Brent didn't move from his spot in the kitchen. "He just hung up. I don't know. You can't come, Brent. Only me."

Brent moved to cradle her in his arms. "You okay? We heard Gabe's voice. That's good. We have to make plans before Tuesday. You did a good job there, getting him to wait. Fast thinking."

"Is he bluffing? Does he know all the cops? Could he have pictures?" She pushed herself away from Brent.

"Wouldn't be hard. Knows anything of computers, he could get access. We can't count on that. We'll need manpower."

Brent stood rooted to the spot midway between the kitchen and family room. Marlo paced the room in front of the expansive windows behind the dining table. "I must do this."

"No, Marlo, you need help. You can't go through this alone."

Doors slammed outside, Brent peered through the door curtains. "I don't believe it!"

Her driveway and the street were crowded with cars. Brent and Marlo stood side by side as his siblings trooped in. They sat, perched, sprawled in every space around the crowded Great Room.

"We're here to help," Alisha announced. "What do you know about Gabe?"

"You know something, don't you? We're here to do

something," said Cameron.

Marlo hesitated. "You can't be there. I'm not to have anyone."

"You've heard from someone. Is Gabe okay?" Cameron turned to his brother. "Do you know anything about this kidnapper?"

"We're family." Alisha touched Marlo's forearm.

Marlo paused. Harrington said *no one*. She glanced at all the intense faces awaiting her word. These were people she loved and trusted. There was a difference between being needy and trusting others. "A man who knew Tony has Gabe." She walked to Brent's side and held his hand. "I'm to meet him on a whaling boat and give him books." Brent held up the books. Marlo continued, "I give him the books and he gives me Gabe."

"So he says," said Cameron. "You have any other details? Is Gabe okay? What are you doing for her safety?"

"We'll have manpower ready to grab him first moment he gives up Gabe."

"You can't." Marlo pulled away from Brent. "You can't bring anyone. " She turned to the group assembled. "He says he has pictures of all Trenton's cops." She pleaded again with Brent. "You can't have anyone on that boat who looks suspicious."

"Does he have the pictures, Brent?" Cameron demanded.

"Don't know. I can't send Marlo on that boat alone. He said vicious things to Marlo. She's not safe."

This immediately brought pandemonium. Voices all at once offered ideas, opinions, and fears. All were directed at Brent.

Alisha walked to Marlo's side. "Don't know how you're handling all this. You okay?"

She nodded. "I heard Gabe's voice today. He's alive. Brent is trying. We've had each other. He's as scared as me. Without each other …" The words stuck in her throat. Her overwhelming need for him flooded her thoughts.

"I have an idea," Cameron announced. The room quieted. "Marlo will be closely observed. She can't do anything, but watch for Gabe, bring the books. Her thoughts will be with Gabe. Brent can't bring on his men." Brent started to protest, but was silenced with a wave of his brother's hand. "But we can. We could be on that boat with her." A stunned silence followed. "We could be the tourists on the boat." A laugh spread among them breaking the tension.

"No guns," stated Brent.

"We could create a diversion for you," Alisha said to her brother. "What is your plan?"

He shook his head. "It's best you don't know. I'll have Curtis brief you this afternoon. I have my work to do," Brent said to Alisha. "You'll stay with Marlo?"

Ericka said, "We'll all be here."

Cameron said, "We'll plan our part."

Brent returned in time for dinner. All others left to their own places. Marlo slept fitfully. Images of Brent, his siblings and words of their plans invaded her thoughts. If they could carry off the plan, she would have Gabe tomorrow.

•

At the sailing vessel, she tried to concentrate on the whaling discussions being conducted by the first mate. She surreptitiously looked around the boat. Where was he? She saw no one from her past, only the friends of her future.

"This is your captain."

She bit her lip to silence her gasp. The voice was Brent's. She studied the captain as he now stood on the outside of the ship's cabin. He didn't resemble Brent. She had shaken hands with this man as she boarded and hadn't recognized him. He was here. Tears welled in her eyes.

A speedboat crossed. The bow nudged too close, slowing the whaling boat. After that, actions happened so quickly, she had no understanding or warning of the activities that followed. Two men leaped from deck close to the captain and held guns to his head. *Brent!* She buried her scream, but added a silent prayer, *Please don't hurt him*. Two men, one armed with a semi-automatic weapon, leaped from the boat to the deck.

Marlo gasped. She did recognize him. The curly black hair, the menacing dark eyes. He motioned her over to him.

"You have the book?"

She slowly pulled a book from the bag and held it behind her back.

"Hand it over."

"Give me Gabe or no book."

"The book." He held out his hand. "Now." She held her bag with the book over the edge near the rumbling motor. "My son, or your bargaining tool is gone."

Harrington studied her face. Marlo didn't flinch. No Gabe. No book. Brent said the book was a bargaining tool. Time stopped. Buoy sounds and the whoosh of the sea broke the silence. Harrington, his henchmen and the boat seemed captured in a picture. Tony had ruled her every move. She only had her instincts here. Marlo never faltered in her eye contact. Stalemate. Her chest felt tight as if squeezed in a vise. She didn't move.

Finally, Harrington waved to the guy on the nearby boat who held up Gabe. His mouth was taped, his eyes wide and hollow. His face scared Marlo the most. Her fingers tightened on the bag. If she could swing it and knock this guy down, but it wouldn't get her Gabe. She silently vowed to pay him back for this moment.

"You vile piece of … " she spat out.

"Careful, honey, I'm still holding him. You'll never see him up close unless you give me that book."

"I give you this when I can touch my son, not until." She held the book out over the water again.

"Get on board. We'll reunite you, then take you to shore near your house. I'll have the book. You'll have your son at home."

She hesitated. Once she got on that boat, she had no one. All her backers beside her were gone. That guy with the automatic weapon would harm anyone who tried to help. She didn't think Brent would just let them go. She couldn't endanger the others. She was on her own to save Gabe.

"You get on first." She motioned to Harrington. "I don't trust you."

Harrington studied the scene. "What are you trying?" He frowned.

"You want the book, get on. I'm not going to let you leave with Gabe. I'll follow, then give you this." She waved the bag, then pulled the book out and waved it in front of him.

Harrington nodded to the other man. "Larry, you make sure

she gets on." He slowly descended the steps to the awaiting boat. Larry straddled the boat side, his gun rested on his thigh. He motioned Marlo to start down the steps while he kept his gun trained on the crowd. As Marlo descended, she paused, stared straight at Brent, then flayed her arms and rocked on the ladder. When Larry bent down to help, she grabbed the gun and dragged downward. Larry, caught off balance, fell overboard. The machine gun dropped from Marlo's hand and fell straight into the grinding paddles beneath the boat.

In an instant, Brent knocked his guard away using the cabin door. The man fell to the deck and remained motionless. Before Brent could get to Marlo's side. Harrington grabbed Marlo by the hair and flung her onto the motorboat, which quickly sped away from the whaling boat. She was alone with Harrington, Gabe and another man. The cohort had a pistol in his belt. Within a small glass cabin, he manned the controls of the boat. He steered as if he were driving a car and never once looked at the dials.

Harrington grabbed the bag off her shoulder and yanked it to him. "Sit over there! What did you think that would accomplish?" He pushed her aside.

She hugged Gabe. She unwrapped the tape and untied the ropes. She crouched near the boat side with Gabe beside her.

"Are you okay?" she whispered just to him. "We must be very careful, but Mommy will get you out of here." She kept her eyes on the two men as she hugged her son. She whispered in his ear so only he could hear. "Brent will help us, too. I'll get us home."

Behind her, the whaling boat became smaller as they moved across the bay. She looked around the bottom of the boat for a weapon. She would need to take out both men.

Harrington engrossed in the books, he didn't look at Marlo or the other man. The man at the helm nervously fidgeted with the wheel. He periodically glanced over the side of the boat. From the movements of both men, Marlo deduced neither was an avid fisherman nor knowledgeable about the Maine coast. Amazed at how much she picked up since living here, she noted the water's current and rough waves.

Harrington's motorboat moved painfully slow through the

waters. These details were in their favor. She searched shore for a route for an escape. The distance from shore did little to help.

"If you go a little to your right," she suggested to the man at the helm, "the coast is a smoother route. We won't bounce on the waves." The crewman appeared green and gladly moved closer to the shore. *Thank you*, she silently prayed. Gabe toyed with the fishing line. At least he was busy so she could concentrate on an escape route.

Gabe moved closer to the two men. She struggled to signal Gabe to come back away from the reach of Harrington. She blinked then stared again at Gabe. With the fishing line, he had woven an intricate pattern around the crewman and around Harrington's feet. She held her breath as Harrington shifted his weight. He didn't notice the lines strung loosely around his feet and a direct line strung across the deck in front of him. The crewman's exit was blocked by line as well. She smiled. Clever child, where had he learned such deviousness? She motioned Gabe over to her side.

The boat spun close to the shore. The rocking of the boat increased as they caught the backwash on the starboard side. The crewman appeared to be adversely affected by the change and looked as if he would like to ditch the boat when he could. A seaman's life was not for him.

"Hey, a page is missing!" Harrington yelled. "Give me the boy! You cheated!"

Harrington lunged at them. The line caught him and he sprawled facedown on the boat. The crewman, seeing his boss in trouble and hearing his swear, jumped to help and also tripped and fell on top of Harrington. Both were entangled in rope and each other's limbs. Harrington swore words that would turn a pirate's hair blue. He snatched for Gabe's coat.

Marlo ground her heel into the Harrington's hand. The crewman struggled. She hit him with an anchor line. She threw a life jacket at Gabe and draped one across her shoulders.

While he put the jacket around him, she threw a spare jacket at the boat gear, sending the boat careening in wide circles. She lowered Gabe in the water and jumped in behind him. Grabbing his jacket line, she pulled him next to her as she swam to shore. *Reach. Come on. Keep your head.* She focused on the boulder formations ahead. *Reach. Kick. Get away.*

Shots rang behind her. Unsure if the shots were aimed at her or the whaling boat, adrenalin racing through her. *Reach.* Gabe's anxious face her spurred her on. *Come on. Reach. We can do this.* Her arms screamed in agony as she struggled to keep up the pace. The futility of each reach brought sobs from within. She fought against the current. *Don't give up. Get Gabe out. Brent.* She prayed he was okay and hadn't been injured in the skirmish she had heard on the boats. *Please God,* she uttered a silent prayer, *don't let me lose him after all this.*

More kicks. She heard the engine roar behind her. The distance of the gunfire and the accuracy were lost in her strokes. Her chest ached with tension and the pressures of the waves. *Kick. Stroke.* She kicked harder. *Don't cry. Don't quit. Move.* The boulder outcropping arose directly before her. Safety. She could hide Gabe. Motorboats couldn't get too close. She could fight. If she saved Gabe, she … *Please, Brent, be okay.*

She grasped the rock, pulled Gabe behind her and lifted him to the edge of one rock formation. She huddled behind the rocks, covering Gabe with her body. She gasped for air. In the bay, power boats mingled together. She stockpiled any small rocks she could find as her only weapons.

"Lie down, Gabe." A boat sped toward them. Unable to make out the driver, she silently chanted her manta. "Make Brent safe. Don't hurt Gabe. Please Brent, we've come this far." She had to believe it would be okay. Hope was her only weapon.

Soon it would be dark. She didn't want to be in the bay in darkness. She was not the Maine native who felt comfortable near the ocean creatures in the darkness. Again she heard gunfire closer. Covering Gabe with her body, she peered over the boulder and waited.

No motors droned nearby. No spouts of water shot from another boat. Stillness echoed across the waters. She methodically breathed in and out to compose herself. "It's okay, we'll be safe as soon as we get home," she assured Gabe and attempted to calm herself.

The air quieted and a deafening, menacing calm followed.

No one came. No boats. No sounds. Darkness closed in around them.

Just awaiting their fate was nothing she could accept. Not anymore. In the last month, she had *acted*. No time to stop. If Brent didn't come find her, it was time to go get him.

"Come on, Gabe. Can you move?" she whispered. He nodded. His eyes were wide with terror. "It's going to be fine. Mommy won't let anything happen to you. We're going home." His silence propelled her actions.

She helped him from their precarious perch and slinging his arms over her back, plunged across the water, dragging him behind her. She swam dragging Gabe behind. Soon her feet hit gritty sand. Her fingers wrapped around the binding pin in Gabe's life jacket. She pulled them to the shore.

She fought to get her footing on the rocky shore. She shrugged out of her life vest and left it on the shore. She held up Gabe as they walked by clinging to the back of his life vest.

Now the darkness enveloped them. They were not visible to boats in the water. She recognized the area as they reached the road. A phone call would bring Brent and she would finally know if he was okay, but she had no cell phone.

She loosened the life vest around Gabe's chest. "We have to walk down this road to our house. I can't carry you. I need you keep up."

Gabe nodded. "Are we going to die?"

"Oh no, Gabe, we're okay. You helped Mommy escape." She leaned down and held him close for a minute. "We're going to be fine. We'll be home soon. You'll be able to sleep in your own bed."

"Will Brent be there?"

Marlo bit her lip. "I hope so. Come on."

Bright lights nearly blinded them when they reached the corner of Dove Street and their road. A search beam glowed eerily atop their heads. A police car! Brent had found them. She grabbed Gabe's hand and scurried forward. The lanky figure stretched from the car was too thin to be Brent. She nearly wilted in disappointment. It wasn't a Trenton police car. She gasped, grabbed Gabe's shoulder and turned.

"Mrs. DeFalco, wait. You're safe. We're all searching for

you. Police from everywhere. I'll take you to Chief O'Neill."

She nearly wept at the words. "Brent, he's okay?"

"Come on, get in. I'll phone in that we found you and take you home." He motioned to the door and as she helped an exhausted Gabe in the back seat, he radioed. "I found them … found them both. We'll be there."

"Brent." She reached for the phone.

He quickly hung up. "No, no madam. They'll let Brent know where you are soon enough." He said nothing. They passed another unfamiliar police car blocking the passage to the cottage. When the man saw the occupants of their car, he nodded and they passed. The police beside her was quiet. He didn't ask of her condition or Gabe's, nor did he offer updates on the search.

He pulled to the back of the cottage, near the bay, turned off his lights. "You go ahead. I'll carry your son." He picked up a groggy Gabe and followed closely behind her. Her gut contracted as she reached the door. Where were Brent's siblings now? Something didn't feel right. She turned to get Gabe.

The policeman shoved her in the door. Hands roughly grabbed her and a bag dropped over her head. Her screams echoed around her ears. She pounded against an unknown chest. Her flailing arms were subdued her by tying her hands behind her. When the bag was removed, she had been shoved into a dining room chair, her hands tied around the back. Harrington stopped before her.

The "cop" stood beside him.

Chapter Thirteen

"Wasn't hard, boss. Mentioned O'Neill just like you said."

Marlo blinked to get her bearings. "Where is my son? Give me Gabe. You have the book."

"Thought you were cute, didn't you? Tying us up on the boat was a mistake. You and the cop O'Neill thought you were so smart to trick me. You weren't that smart." He punched the table next to her. "Where are the other pages?"

"I don't know what you're talking about. Give me Gabe."

"You'll never see him. I'll take him apart before your eyes. Each time you fail to give me what I want, I'll do harm to your son. The missing pages?"

"What pages? I gave you all Tony gave Gabe." Her words choked in her throat. So much lost. Gabe was in Harrington's clutches again. Harrington was safe. Brent had to have been injured. Their plan failed. She failed.

"Except one key series. I want those cards."

"I'm not sure I even know what we're looking for. Tony never informed me—" She never finished the sentence.

Harrington forced her to her feet and close to his chest. The chair still at an abstract angle trailing behind her.

"Tony protected you and held you close. You were always with him. I think, you plan to take over the action and money yourself. I think you're lying. I am not a patient man."

"I don't want anything of his, not his business, not the cards."

"Not his son? We'll get rid of him ..."

"No, leave Gabe alone." Her voice rose. "He never did anything." She slumped back down. The chair at its odd angle dug in her back. Harrington moved toward her.

"Mr. Harrington." A man dressed in greasy overalls with a cap pulled tightly down. "You want me to get rid of the boat now?"

Marlo bit her lip. Cameron was under the hat and overalls. Someone was here. Where was Brent? Had she again led him into danger and led his family as well. She had to take control … somehow. If she could get to Cameron and find out about Brent.

"Where'd you come from? How'd you get here?" Harrington reached in his back pocket.

Cameron shrugged. "You said get rid of the boat once we got here. I wondered if you wanted to do that now? Or later?" Cameron bumbled with his words and shrugged with each phrase as if he had acquired a strange accent.

"Go! I said get rid of it now! That was a half an hour ago. Get it out of sight. Brent and others will recognize it. Go!"

"Then you want me to come back here?"

"No!" Harrington shouted. "Go away. Go get a drink or a new pair of pants." Harrington threw twenty-dollar bills at him. "I paid you to do a job, now go."

Cameron was gone with no sign to Marlo. Brent was alive or Harrington wouldn't worry about him. If Harrington didn't recognize this man was a relative of Brent, then Harrington was as dense as they had thought. She had to rescue Gabe and get out before Brent tried something stupid and this time Brent got hurt.

She held Harrington's arm and shuddered. "Those natives disgust me. So bumbling and unclean."

Harrington smiled down at her. "Soon you won't see them again. Don't miss your lover, the good Mr. O'Neill?"

"He was okay for what I needed him for." She danced her fingers along his arm. "And since you got rid of him … You did get rid of him?"

"No, couldn't get him. But he and his police buddies are on a wild goose chase. Chasing a high speed boat with dummies."

She stifled her reaction to the news. Brent was alive. He was safe. "Clever, aren't you? Tony underestimated your abilities, didn't he?"

"Tony never let me in. Made me the gopher. Not his right

hand guy, but no more. I have Tony's goods and soon I'll be respected … and feared." He tightened the muscle in his arm beneath her fingers.

He was bigger than Tony, but certainly not as cunning. And when you stroked his ego … "I heard Tony talk about you once. He thought you were a threat." Harrington's chest and jaw jutted out. Oh, this worked. "He was so angry at New Year's Eve because he thought I might notice you."

"And you did, didn't you, honey?" His fingers stroked the front of her shirt. Words wouldn't come. She wouldn't have him touch her. The only fingers she ever wanted were Brent's.

A movement on the deck caught her attention. She buried her head on Harrington's chest and wrapped her arms around his neck pulling him to her. She peered beneath his arm. Brent stood on the deck holding Gabe in his arms. Cameron stood next to him as did Patti Closeman. Even with caps pulled down and baggy clothes, she recognized them.

"So honey, you do want me." Harrington started to move away.

She had to keep his attention and give the others a chance to leave. Brent had rescued Gabe. She had to help herself. She leaned into Harrington. Her hands stroked up his chest to his shoulders. "I like your idea of partnership first. But I think I want the details, the *real* details of what you want to do in that room to see if I think they're adequate. Maybe I'll have suggestions of my own." Muffled sounds from outside caught her attention, but her encouraging words had completely distracted Harrington. "We'll look for those pages. We'll start in the bedroom."

She needed a way out. She had to stop him before he actually got her to that bedroom. Her hands roamed around his waist. The gun! She found it in a holster on his back. As she whispered vile descriptions in his ear of bedroom scenes, she cautiously lifted the gun out.

She jumped back and pointed the gun. "Get back from me!" She pointed the gun directly at his heart. "Move away."

Harrington's face registered shock and then transformed to a growing anger. "You think I'm that easy. You shoot me, my men will be here before the sound dies." The men Harrington had on the porch were gone from vision.

She prayed Brent had taken them out when he got in the cottage to get Gabe. "Get back," she snarled. "I shot Tony. I'd think nothing of plugging you." She hid the shaking she felt pervade her body.

"You won't hurt me, honey. You ain't like that."

"Tony thought that, too. He's dead."

"That cop shot Tony,"

"I conned the cop into saying that. He covered for me. That's why I needed him. I had to get rid of Tony and get the stuff." She managed to keep the gun still and put the sneer in her voice. She hadn't realized what acting skills she had.

"Come on, honey, you were just cuddling up next to me. You want me. You were liking what I was describing, let's go in the bedroom and try it out. I can be better than Tony." He moved a step closer.

She couldn't shoot a man. She wasn't going in that room. She glanced toward the porch. No sign of Brent or Gabe. They had to be safe by now.

Harrington used her distraction to lunge and grab her wrist. She whipped her body around and slammed it into his body. She tightened her grip on the gun and fought to keep her hold.

"Let her go!" Brent and two uniformed policemen burst in the room. "Let her go and back up, Harrington. You'll stay alive."

Harrington laughed and wrested the gun free. He held Marlo and pointed the gun at Brent. Not again. Marlo couldn't let this happen again. She sunk her heel into Harrington's shin. She reached up and with a force she didn't know she possessed, Marlo stabbed Harrington's eyes with her fingers. He doubled over and dropped the gun. She sank to the nearby couch as the police handcuffed Harrington and Brent knelt in front of her.

She wrapped her arms around his neck and held on as if her life depended on it. "I was scared. I was afraid for you. I love you, Brent." Unaware of the impact of her admission, she clung to him.

"Gabe is in police station," he whispered. "We'll go to him as soon as …"

"Just hold me, please, Brent," she said. "I know he's okay. I need you. I can go to him later. Just don't let me go, please."

With that plea, he'd hold her as long as he could. Quiet pervaded the cottage after the police took away Harrington.

Marlo leaned back. "Where are your brothers and sisters? Is everyone okay?"

"Yes, fine. They may be lurking outside near the bay. Waiting to see you."

"What happened? Where did they go? What happened after I leaped off the boat?"

"Did you jump? We thought he pushed you. We did send someone to follow his lead."

They walked to his car as he told her the rest. "We need to go to the police station and fill in details. Are you ready? I could call and postpone. I could fix it."

She stopped him. "No, I'm stronger. If you're beside me, I can give a statement."

Before helping her in the car, Brent wrapped his arms around her midriff, she felt his uneven breathing on her cheek. "We searched for you." His arms tightened. "All the boats searched, wave after wave of boats in around the waters. The longer time passed, the worse it got. I was afraid we would find only floating bodies."

She had no desire to leave the security of his arms. "I had no idea if you were safe. Gabe and I hid behind outcroppings in the water. We heard boats ... shots." She shuddered. "I thought Harrington had hurt, maybe killed you. It would have been my fault. I led you into danger again."

"No, not at all." Brent slipped his fingers in her curls and rubbed his cheek with her hair. "You saved many people's lives today. Taking Harrington away from the whaler terrified me. We lost you, but no one on the boat was caught in crossfire. Getting you and Gabe off that boat was ingenious. Harrington would have harmed you both."

As they drove to the station, she described Gabe's fish line attack on Harrington. Brent filled in details of actions as she and Gabe hid.

"How did you know we were back here? And how did you get to Gabe?"

"Mrs. Carlson called the police when she saw car lights on the road and lights go on in your house. Cameron climbed the trellis to the second storey and persuaded Harrington's man to release Gabe. That or take a tumble off the second storey deck."

She gripped Brent's hand. It was over. Gabe was safe. Brent was fine. Her shadows were gone.

After the report at the station, Brent refused to let her and Gabe come back to the cottage after another disaster. Instead, they returned to his house. It was quiet and free of the O'Neill clan.

"Where is your family?"

"Together at Alisha's. Just you and Gabe and me."

Gabe dozed on the couch. He had fallen asleep on the ten minute trip from the police station.

"He's an incredible trooper." Brent sat on the floor and stroked Gabe's head. "We talked to him. He remembered clear details to describe Harrington's men and where they were. He memorized landmarks when the men drove him anywhere in the car. The psychologist who talked with him thought he emerged better than most children would have. Gabe was more worried about us. We'll have to work with him and hopefully his uncertainties will dissipate in time. The biggest trauma he complained about was that Harrington made him play video games for hours."

"If he never wants to go near a video game, I'm sure I'll be thankful. To look at him now, he seems calm. The year hasn't been as hard on him."

"As it has been on his mom." Brent pulled her on the floor beside him. "Let's put Gabe in a bed and work on helping you? Was the year so bad? Will you be alright?"

She snuggled between his legs and curled within the circle of his arms. "Yes."

"Yes to which?" He leaned her back on his arm so she faced him. He gently kissed her lips. The thought he would never be able to kiss her again had destroyed him as they searched for her. He tasted her lips again.

"I want you, Brent. I want to sleep curled up next to you. I thought I would never see you, feel you or kiss you. Kiss me again."

Her kiss was slow and endearing. "Marlo, I think we need to take Gabe to bed before this progresses." He moved away and helped her to her feet then wrapped his arms around her again.

"I thought we were putting Gabe to bed."

"I didn't want the closeness to end. You feel good in my arms."

She sighed and leaned into him. Her fingers instinctively toyed with the hairs around his collar. She loved this closeness. She wanted him as close as she could get him. She didn't care about anything else. She didn't want to think of anything else. "I'll carry Gabe's blanket if you pick him up. I'll follow your lead."

They tucked Gabe in a single bed and both stayed nearby watching Gabe peacefully sleep. A glow covered Marlo and an inward peace enveloped her.

"Come on," Brent whispered and led her from the room to one down the hall. "We'll be able to hear him if he awakens."

At the doorway, Brent swept her up in his arms and carried her across the threshold and to the oversized oak master bed, which dominated the room. He let go. She bounced and disappeared in the depths of a feather bed.

She squealed and laughed a rich, warm triumphant sound. "What kind of bed?"

"My family heirloom. It's been mine since my parents gave it up after the last child was born. It's a great bed for snuggling and spending hours in."

Marlo pushed aside the thoughts of the water, the sight of Harrington's sneer. She wanted to let the touch and the kisses erase the day.

Brent pounced into the bed next to her and reached for the top button on her shirt. "Now let's see what I can do to redeem the day." His eyes raked her body. "What a beautiful woman you are."

He kissed her forehead, her nose, her chin, her belly button. The quick pecks tickled and Marlo's body doubled over to cover her ticklish spots. This only encouraged him. Using the stubble that he had acquired in the last two days, he rubbed his chin under her arms, along her side.

"Brent, Brent!" she squealed in between her giggles. "Please."

"I love to hear your laughter. See your smile. I plan to create days unending that make you do both."

She opened her arms and Brent stretched out beside her. His warmth was just what she needed.

Starting with his belly button, she teasingly tapped her fingers up the middle of his chest. The power and pleasure of hearing him respond, his unabated groans of need spurred her to experiment more. Her hand ran up and down his body. She leaned down and rubbed her cheek along his belly. Her nostrils inhaled the musky, spicy smell that was only Brent's. Her tongue twisted around his belly button savoring saltiness. She couldn't get enough of him. Brent's breathing rhythms changed to a quick intake, almost panting.

The tips of her breasts, then the tips of her hair flirted with the hairs on his chest. She moved down his body keeping contact with his chest. She unbuttoned his jeans and freed his hardness.

"Oh, Marlo, you know what I want now."

The hardness of him in her hand caught her breath. Grasping him in her hand, she nestled between his legs and flicked her tongue along the tip. She felt his short intake of breath.

She watched his face as her mouth and tongue took over her exploration. With his head back, his eyes close Brent's face revealed his mounting passion. She reveled in the sexual tension in him. She smothered the grin and the laughter bubbling inside. The joy of giving him pleasure, witnessing the tremors passing through him, was a rapturous feeling.

"I want you."

Marlo rolled to her back pulling Brent on top of her. He carefully maneuvered himself so his body partially covered hers. His assault of kisses started. As his kisses started at her belly, her hands perused the texture of his back and buttocks.

When his tongue found her most intimate place, her fingers clung to his back. She tried to concentrate enough to not dig her nails in, but his whirling tongue drove away any thought.

"Please, Brent, now." She begged for relief from the passion escalating. As his hand intimately explored the spot his tongue had, he reached to the drawer next to his bed. After slipping the condom on, he moved beneath her and held her hips as he moved within her. "You wanted to be in control. You control the movement."

They rocked together in a tense quest for climax. Both simultaneously peaked and cried out. Their sounds filled the air.

Hours later, Brent, still unable to rest, watched Marlo sleep. She'd said yesterday she loved him. Had she realized her admission, or was it merely an emotional outcry in frenzy of the moment?

Marlo's eyes slowly opened. It was still dark outside. Although only a soft light in the bathroom enabled her to see. The house was quiet. Brent caressed her cheek with his finger. "Hi," she said sleepily. "I dozed. I'm sorry."

She luxuriously stretched across the bed and reached to stroke Brent's chest.

Nestled in his arms with his breath warmly caressing her cheek, Marlo fell back into a contented sleep.

Chapter Fourteen

Marlo awoke to the quiet of Brent's house. The bed was empty beside her. She heard the muffled conversation between Gabe and Brent in a distance. She rolled into the sheets to savor last night. The sheets still had the musky scent of Brent and the faint tantalizing hint of last night's lovemaking.

Unwilling to let go of the sensations remaining from last night, she snuggled back under the sheets. The feel of Brent's hands on her body, the sounds of him as he hit the peak of passion, and the romantic embrace as they slept were memories she didn't wish to end.

Giggles from downstairs brought her out of bed and sleepily she meandered to the landing and looked down on Gabe and Brent sitting at the kitchen table.

"I was scared. The man kept making me play video games. I wanted to fish, go outside. He couldn't cook," Gabe confessed.

Relief passed through Marlo listening to him. If those were the only evils he remembered, he'd be okay. So much in one little boy's life to endure.

"He took my baseball card collection. I've had it my whole life. Will I get it back?"

"I don't think so, but you can start your own collection soon. My brothers collected, maybe each of them will donate a replacement card. I'll give you my collection."

Gabe leaned closer to Brent. "Shouldn't you give that to your son? Things like that get passed down, my dad always said." As soon as he mentioned his father, Gabe's head bowed, his shoulders sagged.

"I don't have a son," said Brent. "But if I did, you would be all the son I could want. I'd like you to have my collection. I'd like to pass mine on down to you." Brent lay his arm around Gabe's shoulders. "I think you were a real brave boy during that whole time. Your mom was worried."

Marlo slipped quietly away and marveled at the wonder of the man, Brent. He had become an important figure in both their lives. She didn't want to lose him. She let the shower run for a minute before stepping in. As she soaped down her body and let the pulse of the shower ease the tension from her shoulders. She smiled recalling a previous shower with Brent's hands rubbing her. His hands. Was that the best of her memories?

The feel of his fingers as he caressed her. Or was it his tongue enticing her? She loved their time in bed. She loved the man. She gasped. Water erratically poured down her face. She made no move to wipe it from her eyes. She made no move. She loved Brent.

The realization hit. A deep sigh followed, then a smile that lit up her whole being. She loved him. She had really known that while on the boulders holding Gabe and worrying about Brent's safety. His safety had been her primary thought. If she had lost him … She loved him. She never wanted to lose him in her life. What now?

The water cascaded down her as she leaned back. Tears formed. Did he love her? He had professed his love and she had spurned him. She had never encouraged him and twice put his life in danger. Could he still care for her? He searched for her, saved her from Harrington's gun. Was that his duty or was it love?

She dressed slowly. How could she tell him she loved him? She had never felt this way, never told someone of her love. She had stated the words to Tony once after a night of elegant dining and dance. Tony had laughed.

As she descended the stairs, the whispered conversation between Gabe and Brent ended. They quickly separated.

"What are we doing today, Mom?" Gabe wiggled from Brent's side. Unable to sit still, Gabe jumped up and down as he talked.

"I'm not sure." Marlo looked at Brent for a lead. Did he

want them to stay?

Brent said nothing.

"I want to go home, Mom." Gabe looked at Brent and winked. "Mom, please I want to go home. I need to go and get my things together. School starts soon."

Marlo stared at the pair. She wasn't prepared to go back. So many memories attached to the cottage. She thought Gabe would want to stay away as well.

"Please, Mommy?"

"Okay, I guess." Brent still said nothing. Nothing about last night, nothing about wanting her to stay with him. She agreed to take Gabe home.

Gabe fidgeted in the car seat, snapping the door lock back and forth.

"Stop that!" Marlo snapped.

Gabe's hand stopped midair. He merely nodded.

She reached out to touch his shoulder. He had grown so much in a short time. So many terrors and changes in his life. In a week, he started school. She needed to focus on Gabe, not her own problems. She needed to discuss the last two weeks, but words failed her.

Together, they unloaded clothing from the car. She fixed a snack, mulling in her mind how she would approach Gabe about his latest trauma.

"Gabe." She stood in the bedroom doorway, his nachos in her hand. "I think it's time I move upstairs. You need space of your own."

"Good idea," he agreed too quickly. "What time is it, Mom?"

"Ten o'clock." She waited until he focused on her, then continued. "You'll need a desk, more of your own toys, a place to work on homework."

"Great. I'll help." He ignored her comments. He was more interested in swinging a yo-yo in dizzy circles.

She stumbled on. "Gabe, I know the last month has been hard, we need to talk about it. In time, you'll forget."

"I love Maine, don't you?" He snapped the yo-yo deftly in a circle, then he bounced up and down and then flipped onto the nearby sling back chair. "We have lots of friends: Jason, Aunt

Alisha, Brent O'Neill."

She stopped her discussion and watched as Gabe sprouted springs and jumped from chair to bed.

"We'll stay in Maine, Mom, right? School starts soon. I can see Jason and Mr. O'Neill. Right? You have friends, like Mr. O'Neill. You do like him?"

"Yes, we'll stay here. You'll have more friends once school starts." She leaned against the door frame. Gabe exhausted her. "Yes, I have friends here."

"Jason's my best friend. He introduced me to Tom, Eddie and Chris." He rattled off the histories of children he'd met. "You won't care if I spend time with them. You need to spend time with friends, Mom."

Marlo sat on the edge of the bed and placed the tray on the floor. "We will probably find a new house." She bridged a new topic. Another change in his life.

"Good idea." He bounced on the bed.

"Sit still." She bit her lip to control her edginess. "I think we need to find our own place." Maybe distance from Brent would help she and Brent figure out their relationship.

Gabe sat on her lap and placed his arm around her shoulders. A rare gesture even for Gabe. "You like Brent a lot don't you, Mommy?"

"Yes." She smiled and hugged Gabe to alleviate the anxiety she heard in his voice. "It's okay to like Brent. I like him. He'll be your friend for a long time."

He wrapped his arms around her neck. "Mom, do you love Brent O'Neill?"

Startled, Marlo unwrapped Gabe's arms and looked into his eyes. What did a seven-year-old know of love? Gabe steadfastly looked back.

"You do, don't you?"

Flashes of Brent shooting Tony, touching her on the picnic, dancing with his family, rescuing her from Harrington ... She thought of how worried she was when she didn't know where he was and how wonderful it felt in his arms. She rubbed Gabe's back. "Yes, I guess I do." The stated admittance was a relief. She did love him.

"Mom. Mom." Gabe tapped her arm. "Mom, what time is

it?"

"Fifteen minutes later. What is your interest in time?"

He shrugged avoiding any eye contact. "Got stuff to do. What are you doing now?"

"Maybe baking. Finding something to eat for lunch."

"You're not going anywhere, right? You don't have to go to the store? I don't want to go anywhere today. Okay?"

"Sure, I guess," she said.

"Can I go outside?"

She watched him bounce on the bed again. His questions had been bizarre and disconnected. Maybe the trauma of the last few days had been too much. No use trying to have any serious discussion. "Will you stay nearby? Eventually, you can ride your bike and explore new places. I'm just not ready yet." She ruffled his hair.

Her fears of the unknown had vanished, but the bad memories lingered. "By tomorrow, we'll go out on your bike."

"I'll stay in the front yard. Bye." He shot out the door.

She picked up the untouched snack and headed to the kitchen. She passed the big door leading to the deck. Below her rock with its ready resting place beckoned. A moment to savor the peace in her life wouldn't hurt and lunch could wait.

Marlo meandered slowly down to her spot by the shore. The autumn breeze touched her cheek. The waves quietly lapped the shore. The cries of the seagulls mingled with the sea air. As she sat, she inhaled the Maine air. She felt better about herself and life than she ever had. Her anxiety passed. She no longer felt as if she had to be watchful. She could enjoy life, enjoy her son and enjoy Brent.

Brent! What could she say? Call him and blurt out, "I love you" now. Blasting out her admission didn't sound tender or loving. How could she tell him? She wanted to tell him, the need rose from deep within her. She needed to admit that. He must still love her. He had demonstrated it in a million ways in the past month.

A candlelight dinner. A plan formed. Just the two of them. She'd send Gabe to Alisha's. Soft music. Dinner. Then she'd say, "I love you, Brent. I want a lifetime of you."

"Mom!" Hearing Gabe's frantic shriek, she leaped to her

feet and raced up the hill to the front. *Not again, please not again.* She stumbled to the front as a procession of cars lined the street. Gabe stood in the middle of the yard, unharmed, safe and grinning.

She stared in disbelief at her son, dancing with glee. She gaped at the arriving entourage of cars. The entire O'Neill gang, complete with newlyweds, Ericka and Ian, disembarked and formed a pathway from the cars and along her walkway. Each moved silently. Marlo, dumbfounded, remained motionless.

A familiar jeep flew down the street, a trail of dust following his speeding vehicle. Brent stopped in front of her walkway. Dressed in black jeans and a dark turtleneck, the sight of him stirred desire in Marlo. He stood at the head of the pathway created by his siblings. He smiled. Marlo felt lightheaded and confused.

"The flowers," Gabe yelled. Brent nodded at Gabe, walked to his Jeep. When he turned back he carried a large bouquet of red roses. He walked slowly to Marlo. Gabe skipped to his side.

"Hello," he said softly. A tender, satisfied smile crossed his lips. His gaze held promise. Marlo, unsure and bewildered by the events unfolding before her, smiled tentatively. An awkward silence followed. None of the O'Neill crew made a sound.

"Are these for me?" Marlo asked touching the flowers.

"Here." Brent thrust the flowers in her arms and knelt on one knee in front of her, which caused a murmur of satisfaction form his sisters.

"I once told you, I'd do this better," he began.

"What?" A blush rose to Marlo's cheek.

"Will you marry me, Marlo?"

"She loves you!" Gabe blurted. "She told me."

Gabe's admission brought shouts of encouragement from the males behind them.

"Marry me." Brent's eyes were full of tenderness. Then turned to Gabe. "You're part of this, too." He slipped his arm around Gabe and the two looked at her for answers.

Marlo, so overwhelmed by Brent and Gabe linked arm and arm, couldn't get a sound out. But the thought of being forever with Brent, of awakening with his arms around her and with sharing each moment with him generated her response.

She leaped into his arms not waiting for Brent to react. "Yes!" she shouted to the heavens as she, Brent and the flowers landed in an indistinguishable heap on the ground.

The gang watching this enactment shouted and clapped. Gabe dove in the pile of body parts on the ground. Marlo rolled to a sitting position dusting the grass and pine needles from her clothes. Brent shakily stood up.

Gabe grabbed the roses, gently shook them and handed them to his mother. "You keep these."

"No, Gabe, you hold them and when we go in, put them in water." She reached for Brent's hand and pulled herself to a standing position.

"No, Mom, they're important." Gabe leaned toward her and whispered. "The ring. Look in the ribbon."

"What?" She held the flowers above her head. A ring box dangled from the bow. "Oh!" Taking the red velvet box in her hand, she looked at Gabe. "How did you know?"

"We planned this yesterday and this morning," Gabe said.

"Open it." Brent touched her hand, then pointed to the box. Gabe and Brent stood expectantly before her.

Inside was a ring. A ring uniting her with a person who loved her and wanted her. A love she never expected to find.

Brent lifted her right hand, gently stoked the top of her hand, leaned to kiss her then slipped the ring on her finger. "Beats a ring in the shower stall," he whispered so only she could hear.

Stepping around Gabe, he pulled her into his warm, firm embrace. She snuggled closer nestling her head beneath his chin. She wrapped her arms around him. This was heavenly and she could do this forever.

"Will you?" Brent leaned back away from her. "Will you marry me and love me forever?"

"Forever." She snuggled closer to Brent and each reached out and pulled Gabe into their circle of arms. The O'Neill siblings crowded closer.

•••

Reece Brett

Reece Brett lives in New Jersey with her own romantic hero, her husband. To escape the rewarding yet chaotic life of a blended family with six children, Reece and her husband kayak. Reece is a staff writer and freelance photographer for two arts magazines in New Jersey. Although she has published stories, articles and children's books, her lifelong dream has been to publish a novel.

www.ReeceBrett.com